D1559861

For

Aunty Lily
and other delightfully perverse stories

The people of
Evanston. Enjoy!
Jennifer Munro
November 2017

Aunty Lily

and other delightfully perverse stories

Jennifer Munro

Parkhurst Brothers Publishers
MARION, MICHIGAN

www.parkhurstbrothers.com

Parkhurst Brothers books are distributed to the trade through the Chicago Distribution Center, and may be ordered through Ingram Book Company, Baker & Taylor, Follett Library Resources and other book industry wholesalers. To order from Chicago Distribution Center, phone 1-800-621-2736 or send a fax to 800-621-8476. Copies of this and other Parkhurst Brothers Inc., Publishers titles are available to organizations and corporations for purchase in quantity by contacting Special Sales Department at our home office location, listed on our website. Manuscript submission guidelines for this publishing company are available at our website.

Printed in the United States of America

First Edition, 2016

2016 2017 2018 2019 2020 16 15 14 13 12 11 10 ... 6 ... 2 1

Library of Congress Cataloging-in-Publication Data

Names: Munro, Jennifer, author.
Title: *Aunty Lily : and other delightfully perverse stories* / Jennifer Munro.
Description: First hardback edition. |
Marion, Michigan : Parkhurst Brothers Publishers, 2016.
Identifiers: LCCN 2015049221 (print) | LCCN 2016001183 (ebook) |
ISBN 9781624910722 (hardcover : acid-free paper) | ISBN 9781624910739 (ebook) |
Subjects: | BISAC: FICTION / Humorous. | FICTION / Literary. | FICTION /Contemporary Women.
Classification: LCC PR6113.U67 A6 2016 (print) | LCC PR6113.U67 (ebook) | DDC 823/.92--dc23
LC record available at http://lccn.loc.gov/2015049221

Parkhurst Brothers Publishers believes that the free and open exchange of ideas is essential for the maintenance of our freedoms. We support the First Amendment to the United States Constitution and encourage all citizens to study all sides of public policy questions, making up their own minds. Closed minds cost a society dearly.

Cover and interior design by   Linda D. Parkhurst, Ph.D.
Proofread by   T. Percival Lamont
Acquired for Parkhurst Brothers Inc., Publishers by: Ted Parkhurst

062016

This book is dedicated to my mother and father,

Barbara and Albert Blount,

who taught me to laugh and love in equal measure.

Contents

Preface   7

Map of Thurmaston   8

The Wicket Gate   11

A Real Friend   25

Gone Fishing   35

Aunty Lily   44

The Revenge of Stuart Smith   48

The Arrival   60

The Adventure   65

Sundays   82

Home Delivery   95

Paying Homage   106

Earnest   125

Read My Lips   135

The Fisher King   148

Acknowledgements   162

Reading Group Extras   164

Author's Essay   165

Biography   172

Q&A with Jennifer Munro   175

Preface

AUNTY LILY AND OTHER DELIGHTFULLY PERVERSE STORIES is a collection of fictional stories harvested from childhood memories, adult experiences, and the general flotsam and jetsam of family folklore. They are based on oral performance pieces: stories I tell before live audiences; therefore, their construction and form differ in nature from literary tales. The stories are written in the first person and are an artful blend of fact and truth, memoir and autobiography.

In looking back, memories and the family stories we traded as oral currency leap vividly to life in my mind. I remember them all in exacting detail, and it is from a combination of these real and retold events that my stories spring. The truths I am trying to share are not earth-shattering; they are straightforward insights, which I hope confirm what it means simply to be human.

As you read these stories, may you find yourself pausing to say, "Oh, that reminds me of when...." Stories trigger stories; I hope the memories they evoke bring an occasional tear and an abundance of smiles.

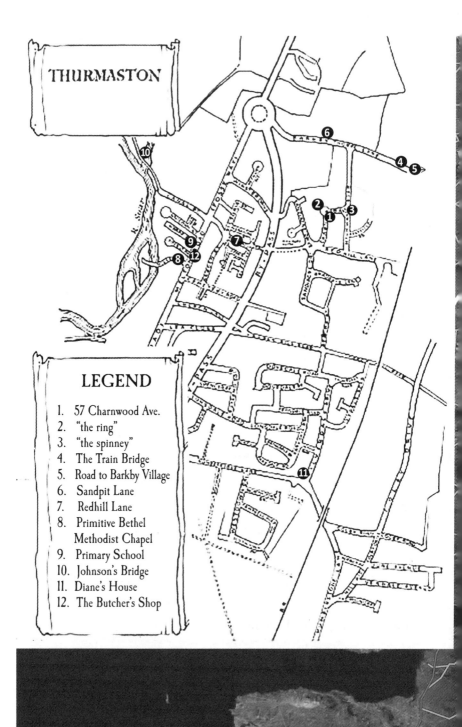

THURMASTON

LEGEND

1. 57 Charnwood Ave.
2. "the ring"
3. "the spinney"
4. The Train Bridge
5. Road to Barkby Village
6. Sandpit Lane
7. Redhill Lane
8. Primitive Bethel
   Methodist Chapel
9. Primary School
10. Johnson's Bridge
11. Diane's House
12. The Butcher's Shop

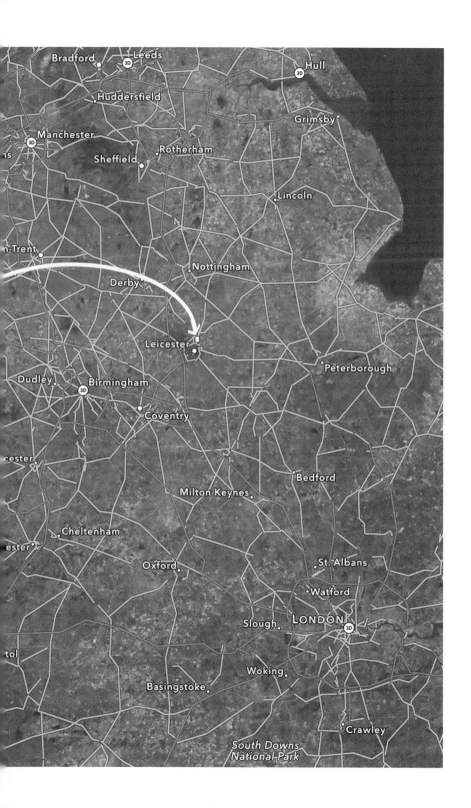

The Wicket Gate

I WAS TO BE IN MISS TURNER'S FIRST FORM CLASS at Thurmaston Church of England Primary School. Miss Turner was tall, imposing, and brown. Her brown hair was cut in two perfectly straight lines: one at the front and one at the back. What's more, it never moved. Whenever she turned her head, it moved with her like an obedient helmet. Her eyes were probably brown too, but we could never tell because she wore thick-lensed glasses that reflected the light, bringing to her face a look of constant, sightless surprise. She wore brown sweaters, brown tweed skirts, thick brown woolen stockings, and sensible brown walking shoes.

But the things that fascinated us about Miss Turner were her bosoms. At first glance Miss Turner appeared to be flat-chested. This was because many years since, her generous bosoms had dropped down to waist level where they were prevented from further descent by a sturdy, brown leather belt. Just as her hair stayed still so it was that her bosoms, at the slightest provocation, delighted to roll and romp around her middle like two joyful, Jell-O® filled balloons.

I arrived at school that first morning breathless with anticipation. I was in the first form and I was going to learn to read. My debut in infant school the year before had not been an impressive one. I had not yet learned all of the letters of the alphabet and those I did know came out backwards, upside down and—despite all my efforts—insisted on working their way from the right hand side of the page to the left. But I had will power, I had determination, and I had Miss Turner. I decided she'd have me sorted out by lunch time.

When the bell rang, we formed a line and filed into the dark, cavernous stairway that led to the assembly hall. We trod upon the wooden steps, which were buckled like so many sway-backed horses by the countless generations of children who had trodden before us. We marched into the hall where after prayers and hymns and a speech of welcome from Mr. "Pop" Precious, the headmaster, we, the chosen few, followed Miss Turner's bouncing balloons from the hall. Miss Turner stopped at the classroom door and folded her arms above her bosoms, trapping them into a brief moment of stillness and waited while we stood behind our desks. I stood next to Sylvia Simpson. Sylvia was a tall, pale, quiet girl who liked to faint ... a lot.

Smiling, Miss Turner bounced into the room—her

bosoms released into an agitated state of excitement. "Sit down, my Pilgrims, sit down." Miss Turner sat down in a large, comfortable chair at the front of the class, took out a huge book and began to read.

> So I walked through the wilderness of this world, I lighted on a certain place where there was a den, and laid me down in that place to sleep; and as I slept, I dreamed a dream. I dreamed, and behold, I saw a man clothed with rags standing in a certain place, with his face from his own house, a book in his hand, and a great burden upon his back. I looked, and saw him open the book, and read therein; and as he read, he wept and trembled; and not being able longer to contain; he brake out with a lamentable cry, saying, "What shall I do?"[1]

Miss Turner paused and looked at each one of us pointedly. There was no doubt in my mind she saw each of us as that poor wretch standing before her with the burden of our own ignorance heaped upon our backs. I wriggled uncomfortably in my seat wondering if she could see at a glance that my burden was larger and heavier than most.... She did! She turned directly to me, pointed through the window, and said, "Pilgrim, do you see yonder wicket gate?" Her thick-lensed glasses directed her gaze straight into my heart, and I knew she was really asking, "Do you see yourself learning to read?"

I tried to imagine myself picking up a book. I tried to imagine the letters on the page behaving long enough to reveal their mystery to me, but I could see no such wicket

---

1   From John Bunyan's *The Pilgrim's Progress*, London, 1678.

gate. My face flushed an uncomfortable throbbing red. Not being able to contain myself any longer, I broke out with a lamentable cry saying, "What shall I do? Oh, what shall I do?" In answer, she looked out of the window and pointed across the fields. "Pilgrim, do you see yonder shining light?" The sunlight reflected off her glasses, two beams of light stretching into the distance. Too awed to speak, I nodded dumbly. Miss Turner threw her arms and bosoms around me and cried, "Keep that light in your eye, and go directly thereto, so shalt thou see the wicket gate."

Just as I had expected! All this and it wasn't even lunch time yet!

After lunch, Miss Turner wrote in a beautifully neat hand all the letters of the alphabet, which we had to copy. It was then that the enormity of my burden was revealed. Miss Turner took one look at the delinquent efforts of my pencil, and her response was immediate. "Pencils down!" she roared. Everyone quickly obeyed except for Sylvia who did so, but slowly. She did everything slowly ... she even fainted slowly.

"Line up by the door."

We did so and Miss Turner took us outside and through the boy's playground. I'd never been in the boy's playground before; Sylvia almost fainted. Ms. Turner turned to me and said, "Jennifer, you're a fine sturdy girl."

"Yes Miss Turner."

"You will be the Sylvia Catcher. When Sylvia faints, you will catch her."

My first position of responsibility! "Yes, Miss Turner," I beamed. Steven Pringle glared. He was in love with Sylvia and wanted desperately to catch her himself. Ignoring him, I moved over to Sylvia protectively, and we continued out of the playground and into the field beyond.

"Run, Pilgrims, run," yelled Miss Turner. "Look for that which begins with the letter 'A'."

We ran off squealing with delight. I kept close to Sylvia, steering her away from the cow pies. Cow pies made Sylvia faint. We found an ant's nest. I squished two and put them into my pocket. Sylvia was far too sensitive to have dead ants in her pocket.

"Now look for something beginning with the letter 'B'," shouted Miss Turner. In this way we hunted for objects beginning with as many letters of the alphabet as we could. When we got back to class, we spread our treasures on our desks and Miss Turner gave us each a piece of paper and a pot of glue. Working from the top of the page and from left to right, we had to stick our treasures in alphabetical order in rows across the page. When everyone was busy, Miss Turner came over to my desk and wrote in indelible ink on the nails of my index fingers an "L" for left and an "R" for right. She watched while I worked, her glasses shining two beams of light onto the page.

And so it was that every day we went on pilgrimages down to the river to catch sticklebacks and frogspawn, leaves, wild flowers, and unusual fungi. When we returned to the classroom, sometimes Miss Turner would choose three items and we had to make up a story involving all three objects, which we told to one anther or we'd act them out. Miss Turner put me in charge of the nature table, and I had to display the things we found always in the same way, starting at the top of the table and working from the left to the right, from the left to the right. Since everything was placed thus in neat rows, Miss Turner showed us an easy way to keep a count of our treasures—multiplication she called it.

And all the time we were engaged in these activities, Miss Turner sat in her easy chair and read to us from John Bunyan's *The Pilgrim's Progress*. Christian had fallen in with Obstinate and Pliable and as a result of their counsel was now floundering around in the Slough of Despond. I knew just how he felt. These pilgrimages were all very well and good, but I was no closer to the wicket gate than I was at the beginning of the year. Everyday when we passed the other first form window, we saw the other kids, brows wrinkled, laboring over their first reading books sounding out letters and words.

It was almost the end of October and we hadn't even opened a book yet! I began to suspect that Miss Turner didn't really know what she was doing. I began to think the scores of children who had gone before us loved Miss Turner precisely because she liked pilgrimages more than she liked forcing children to read. The fears and doubts engulfed me and I floundered around in a Slough of Despond of my own creation.

My spirits revived a little with the onset of winter. Now that it was too cold to go out, maybe she would actually teach us to read, but no such luck! Instead, we learned how to sew! Both boys and girls were given small square table mats which we dutifully embroidered in rows working from the top and from the left to the right, from the left to the right. I was sick of left to right—even I knew my left from my right and no longer needed the indelible reminders on the nails of my index fingers!

And still Miss Turner read to us. Poor Christian had no sooner crawled out of the Slough of Despond but had fallen in with Mr. Worldly Wise. *Could it be that Miss Turner was Ms. Worldly Wise,* I thought, leading us all like Christian toward the Village of Morality and toward destruction?

Our destruction took the form of large lumps of wet clay, which were dished out to every pilgrim. While the other first form class was well into its second reader, we made animals, cars, and trucks. Stephen Pringle made a heart for Sylvia. He was the son of the local butcher. It looked like a real heart with valves and ventricles and blood. Sylvia took one look at it and fainted in slow motion at Stephen's feet. He was thrilled! After that Miss Turner put her foot down and insisted that we all make long skinny worms, which we had to shape into the letters of the alphabet. We painted them back and front and hung them up to dry. Then, some of the pilgrims made them into words and put them under the things we had made.

I tried! Every day, I tried to remember which way round the letters needed to go to form words, but some still insisted on coming out upside down or backwards. One day when I arrived at school, Miss Turner had made me my very own set of letters out of sandpaper. Since they were rough on one side and smooth on the other, I knew which way round they went. Miss Turner divided us into two teams, and we had to form words out of the sandpaper letters. The other team, blindfolded, had to guess what the words were. Stephen Pringle made the word F-A-R-T. FART! I guessed what it was, and Miss Turner wasn't even angry one bit.

And still Ms Turner read to us. Good news for Christian, too. At last, he had been rescued from the Village of Morality by Evangelist and was back on the straight and narrow path where Interpreter took him firmly by the hand and led him the last few treacherous steps leading to the wicket gate, which flew open immediately allowing Christian to pass through. He stood before the cross where a golden light shone round about him. Suddenly, his great burden fell from his back. Then dressed in fine raiment, Christian set his face toward the Celestial City.

And just like Christian, many Pilgrims in the class had also found the wicket gate. They were able to go to the book shelf, select a book, and read with an ease that I could only envy. Miss Turner no longer referred to them as Pilgrim but proudly called them Christian. Oh, but when would I see the wicket gate? When would I start to read? That's what I wanted to know!

"Soon, my Pilgrim," said Miss Turner—her bosoms drooping even more in sympathy—"When you are least expecting it, Interpreter will thunder into your path and lead you directly to the wicket gate. It will fly open without the slightest effort on your part, and you will find that you are able to read. That's how it happens, my pilgrim. That's how it always happens." Well, I knew Miss Turner was a woman of her word, and so all I had to do was to keep my wits about me and my eyes wide open.

However, it was the springtime. The year was winding down and I knew being able to read the word "fart" was not sufficient to get me to the wicket gate. I realized that I might still be a pilgrim going into second form. Undaunted by this failure, one bright day Miss Turner went to the window and announced that the weather was perfect for a pilgrimage. We gathered up our fishing nets and jam jars and—like Christian soldiers—marched out of the school and into the main street. This was unusual. Usually we set off across the fields, but today we were going to Johnson's bridge to the waterfall, and through the village was the quickest way to get there.

When we arrived, the Christians threw off their shoes, scattering their socks like flakes of snow, and splashed into the icy water. Miss Turner disappeared behind a bush and peeled off her stockings. Her white cod fish feet doubled in size as she paddled into the river, her bosoms settling themselves into a ready made, inflatable rubber ring should flotation become necessary.

I wanted to join in, but my heart just wasn't in it. The burden of my ignorance rested too heavily upon my back.

As I sat idly watching the Christians having boat races down the waterfall and working out complicated sums involving time and speed, a sudden fear gripped me. Without realizing it, I was allowing sloth and idleness to engulf me; a pilgrim needed always to be on her guard. I lifted up my burden and scanned the horizon searching for the ever elusive wicket gate, but all I could see was the constant flicker of sunlight flashing off Miss Turner's glasses.

Then, I took off my shoes and socks and splashed into the water towards Sylvia. She had caught a fish—she could catch them, but she couldn't touch them or she fainted. I plopped it into the jam jar. By this time, however, the Christians' feet had turned blue, and it was time to go. We sat on the river bank, dried our feet as best we could, and put on our shoes and socks. We made drawings of the fish we had caught before we released them, and then lined up ready for the march back to school. We filed over Johnson's bridge and along the fence by Farmer Johnson's field. Something was going on. On the far side of the field, Mr. Johnson was standing by a horse box that belonged to the veterinarian. The farmer and the veterinarian were locked in animated conversation. In the field there was a lone cow.

"It must be sick," concluded Miss Turner, and she lined us up along the fence to watch what was going to happen. The cow rather than looking sick, however, frisked and frolicked around the field with an abandon similar to that of Miss Turner's bosoms. The vet' and the farmer started to gesticulate wildly, and though we couldn't hear clearly what they were saying, it was obvious to me they wanted us gone. It may have been that the distance was too great or she couldn't see properly because of the sun shining into her eyes, but Miss Turner obviously neither saw nor heard and instead of leading us away, responded with an enthusiastic, but inappropriate, "Hallooooo!"

The two men, anxious to be about the business at hand, shrugged and walked back to the horse box. Miss Turner was well known in the village for her unusual educational methods. They must have decided she knew what she was doing. Then the vet' opened the trailer door while the farmer cautiously undid the five-barred, wooden gate. The bull, a huge animal of staggering proportions, charged out of the trailer with such force that the gate was knocked out the farmer's hands and flew open wide. I stared hard at that gate—it was the first gate I had seen all year, and I recognized it instantly. It was a five barred, wooden wicket gate. Instantly, I gathered my wits about me and kept my eyes fastened on Interpreter, for that's who I knew it to be. Interpreter thundered into the field and stood heaving and snorting, steam shooting from both nostrils, his tail lashing backwards and forwards in an agitated manner. The effect on the cow was immediate. She set up a bellowing the like of which I had never heard before. It was guttural and primal. The effect on Miss Turner was also immediate. She, too, let out a cry that was both guttural and primal, and for the first time that year her bosoms were perfectly still. They sat rigidly to attention, as O. Henry would say, like "two setters at the scent of a quail.[2]" Then I remembered my position of responsibility. I turned to Sylvia ready to catch her when she fainted, but there was no need. For the first time that year her eyes were shining and her cheeks were an unusually healthy pink!

Then the bull charged after the cow, dust and grass flying. The cow set off in a half hearted attempt at escape. The bull reared again and again as the cow swerved and jumped and frolicked, seemingly oblivious to any threat the bull may have posed. There was no doubt in our minds just who was in charge in this game. The bull bellowed in frustration and when it seemed he was ready to burst, the cow dug in all four hoofs and stood stock still. The bull, unable to contain his momentum, crashed into her rear end in an undignified manner. Unperturbed, he managed to rear up once more and this time his front hoofs rested squarely on the back of the now cooperative cow.

"Bull's eye!" Mr. Johnson roared, and as quickly as the whole thing started, it ended with the bull following on the cow's heels like a lamb that had narrowly escaped the slaughter.

"That'll give 'em something to write about," yelled the farmer this time cupping his mouth with both hands.

Miss Turner, rendered incapable of speech for the moment, managed only to smile weakly. She relaxed her grip

---

2   From *The Gift of the Magi*, written by O. Henry, (William S. Porter), 1905.

on the fence and her bosoms dropped back into their usual position where they rolled dreamily around her middle like waves gently lapping against the shore. We stood in line once more and thoughtfully followed the ebb and flow of their tide. When we reached the street, Miss Turner seemed to revive. "Let's sing!" she cried. This was unusual, but a song did seem necessary to relieve the tension that still gripped the orderly line.

Glad that I live am I;
That the sky is blue;
Glad for the country lanes,
and the fall of dew.

After the sun, the rain,
After the rain, the sun;
This is the way of life,
'Till the work be done.[3]

The postmaster waved to us out the post-office window, pedestrians stopped to laugh and stare, but my heart beat in time with the rhythm of our singing. To think that I had seen the wicket gate and of all places in Farmer Johnson's field! I threw it open wide amazed at how easy it was. I looked down Thurmaston Main Street where I could see the small cross on the top of the school, and I felt the weight of my burden fall

---

3   From the hymn "The Wayside Lute" by Lizette W. Reese, 1909.

effortlessly from my back. The sunlight flashed off Miss Turner's glasses surrounding me in golden raiment.

As we filed in through the main entrance of the school and went by the headmaster's study, I saw the commemorative brass plate on the wall. I read the inscription clearly and loudly: "Thurmaston Church of England Primary School, established in 1844 by the Thurmaston Parish Council." I was amazed at how obedient the letters were. Miss Turner smiled and as we passed by the other first form classroom where they were still laboring over their readers, Miss Turner changed the song and we filed into our classroom singing "Onward Christian Soldiers." I sat in my seat a Christian ready to set off with all the other Christians toward our own individual Celestial Cities.

A Real Friend

FOR THE PURPOSES OF SPORTS DAY at our primary school, the village was divided into two factions: the North and the South. The scrappy, working class kids lived in the North and those children who rose to the dizzy heights of the middle classes lived in the South. We Northerners occasionally won our sporting events by using sheer grit and determination— and by cheating when we could get away with it. The blue ribbon identifying those of us from the North and the red for the South were largely superfluous; we Northerners wore our ragged school PE uniforms and holey plimsoles, flimsy, insubstantial canvas shoes, while those from the South sported brand new shorts, red T shirts, and real athletic shoes—some even wore spikes. Despite our occasional cheating, we never really stood a chance.

We also formed our friendships as if an invisible line

had been drawn down the middle of the village—those of us who lived in the predominantly government-owned council houses that made up the bulk of the North rarely made friends with those from the South, who lived in detached houses and bungalows, which their parents actually owned and where they grew flowers instead of potatoes.

However, when I was ten and in my final year in primary school, the impossible occurred. Diane Giannopoulos, who heralded from the South, looked upon me with something resembling kindness and invited me to tea after school! Dianne Giannopoulos was a small, dark-skinned, brown-eyed somber girl whose dark silky hair was cut all one length that ended in a straight line just below her ears. To keep it from falling across her face, she wore a partial pony tail tied at the side of her head by a large, brown satin bow. Though unremarkable in many ways, she was surrounded by an aura of hopeless sophistication. This was on account of the fact that her mother and father were divorced—which would have been a scandal had not her father—a wealthy, mysterious foreigner—left the family well provided for. Diane and her mother still lived in their large detached house that had an automatic washing machine and a telephone, forms of technology that would take years to arrive on Charnwood Avenue where I lived.

At my house, Diane's invitation was heralded by total disbelief, and on the day of the tea party necessitated a great deal of early morning scrubbing until I glowed an unhealthy salmon pink. The night before, my mother had set out a freshly laundered white shirt—usually one did for the entire week—and she brushed and ironed my navy blue pleated skirt—a hand-me-down worn shiny by years of use.

The event exceeded all my expectations. When we arrived, Diane's mother had just come out of the bath tub—at four o'clock on a Wednesday afternoon! In my family, all six of us—one after the other beginning with my parents—shared the same bath water once a week on Saturday nights so that in the unlikely event we might decide to go to church the next morning we would not be found wanting. Not only that, but Diane's mother wore a skimpy, bright red dressing gown made of some sort of silky material that barely reached to her knees and failed to disguise the fact that she was completely naked beneath. By contrast, my mother always wore a thick, flannel affair that succeeded in concealing the fact that she was human let alone there might be a female body beneath it.

Mrs. Giannopoulos's eyes flickered over me from top to toe, taking in the frayed cuffs of my now ink-stained shirt and shiny skirt, and emitted an exasperated sigh. Then, with a dismissive wave of her cigarette, she bade us wash our hands while she disappeared into the kitchen.

The bathroom was a revelation: pearly white tiled walls, thick, plush bathroom mats that swallowed my feet as hungrily as sinking sand, and a low, pink—pink!—toilet, on which my granddad might have been able to lower himself but never get back up again. It had a matching a pink hand basin and bath tub. In my mind, I contrasted the tiny delicate toilet to our monstrous lav' with its black water tank on the wall above and long chain and handle for flushing—technology we considered revolutionary compared to the outhouses we had been used to. But most shocking of all: there was no evidence to suggest that someone had just taken a bath, which meant that they had *two* bathrooms! For a moment, I could hardly take in the magnitude of this alien reality! Recovering only slightly, I washed my hands and followed Diane to what she called the dining room where we sat down to eat.

Mrs. Giannopoulos arrived carrying a large tray—she hadn't even bothered to get dressed to prepare the tea! I was dizzy with delight!

Then, rendered speechless, I gazed open-mouthed at the food she had prepared: tinned spaghetti on toast and as many Kit-Kat® bars, still wrapped in their silver foil and orange wrappers, as we wanted for dessert—store bought luxuries which we Blount kids raised on solid, home made fare coveted with almost a biblical passion. I gazed longingly at the mountain of sweet temptation and resisted a momentary impulse to stuff a few chocolate bars into my school satchel! They would hardly be missed.

Remembering my manners, I recovered somewhat and said, "Thank you, Mrs. Giannopoulos." The words did the breast stroke in the pond that had gathered in my mouth. Mrs. Giannopoulos gave another dismissive wave of her cigarette and disappeared into the hallway where soon she began to murmur and laugh quietly into the telephone.

I waited until Dianne picked up her knife and fork and watched as, with an air of studied indifference, she cut off a tiny piece of toast and popped it disinterestedly into her mouth. I tried to follow her example, but I was already a lost cause. One delicious tangy whiff of tomato sauce thrust all notion of polite restraint aside. Grabbing my knife and fork, I bent my head to the task and shoveled in great mounds of toast and spaghetti one after the other until only a few singed crumbs and a smear of orange sauce remained. With a sigh of satisfaction, I sat back in my chair and looked at Diane, who was staring at me with a sort of horrified fascination.

"I didn't have much lunch," I smiled sheepishly, noting that she had hardly eaten a thing.

As if she couldn't imagine it possible I could eat another morsel, she announced, "We'll have dessert later," and for a moment I was bereft.

"We're going outside to play," she informed her mother.

Another dismissive wave of the cigarette and an admonition not to get dirty sent us on our way.

The back garden consisted of a neat lawn as smooth as green velvet surrounded by a wide spacious border of blooming flowers. It was dominated by a towering tree that sheltered a small, neat play house. A garden shed, looking almost as neat as the little house, hid behind a flowering bush.

"Let's climb the tree," I yelled.

"I'm not allowed to climb trees," Diane declared, as if

that settled the matter.

"Oh."

"We'll play dress up!" Diane insisted in such a way I knew I had little choice in the matter.

I groaned when I saw the array of fairy princess dresses that hung on tiny hooks inside the play house. In no time at all, Diane transformed herself into a yellow princess, and then with a firm efficiency that fairly took my breath away, she grabbed a pink confection and thrust it over my head. Before I knew what had happened, I was a fairy. A gold tiara completed my humiliation—and I wished that the privet hedge surrounding the garden was a little taller to keep prying eyes away.

Diane pretended to prepare tea and poured it into the diminutive china cups upon the small table. I sat my over-sized self in the undersized chair and did my best to appear as if I were enjoying myself—as Diane evidently was. But, after sipping numerous cups of air, even she began to lose interest. "Let's play something else," I suggested. "Do you have any stilts?"

Diane looked startled. "No."

"What about snobs or marbles?"

"No."

"How about conkers?"

"What?"

"Never mind!" I wracked my brains. Then, remembering the smooth, green lawn, I suggested, "We could play stretch if I'd brought my knife."

She didn't hesitate. "I bet there's one in the shed. My daddy left all his tools behind." She ran off to investigate and returned flushed with success and handed me a substantial pocket knife. Though it was somewhat stiff, I managed to open up the impressive blade. Then, still dressed as fairies, we skipped across the grass.

Diane had a momentary hesitation. "I'm not sure my mother would approve of playing with knives," she said, glancing nervously toward the house.

I thought to myself that none of the kids in my neighborhood would approve of my fairy outfit either, but I didn't say that. "Has she ever said you can't play stretch?"

"Well, no but ..."

"Well, then, there's no problem. It's fun. You'll see."

I showed her how to hold the knife and throw it in such a way that it stuck into the velvet lawn. She tried it a few times, seeming to enjoy the weight of the knife and the satisfying sound it made when the blade sank into the soil. "Not bad!" I exclaimed and she beamed.

I explained the rules of the game, which were simple. We had to stand facing one another and taking turns throw the knife just a few inches to the right or left of one another's foot, and then we had to remove the knife and move our foot to that spot. If the knife failed to stick into the ground, you didn't have to move your foot. If you threw the knife too far, you lost that turn, and if you threw it too close, you might lose a toe, but nobody ever had.

Gradually, our feet would get further and further apart until we couldn't stretch any more and one of us would fall down, which meant you lost the game. We began to play and for a first timer, Diane was doing brilliantly. Thoroughly engrossed in the game, she gripped the knife and threw it as if her life depended on it. Only once or twice did the knife fail to stick into the ground.

Soon, both our feet were getting wider and wider apart, and we were both wobbling dangerously. Diane was laughing out loud—something I'd never heard her do before. "This is fun!" she cried as she threw the knife with deadly accuracy to within an inch of my right foot.

"Watch it. Not too close!" But I couldn't help laughing, too. I pulled out the knife, covered the place with my foot, and started to wobble in earnest. Diane laughed even louder, but then I had my turn and she, too, was struggling to stay upright. Suddenly, quick as a whippet, she shot forward and pushed me over. As I went down, I took hold of the big, brown satin bow in her hair and gave it a tug. With her hair spilling over her face, she fell down on top of me. We went rolling away from the knife, across the lawn, a human barrel of pink and yellow tulle and navy blue serge, and across the flowery border into the dirt.

Heedless of our fairy outfits or of our school uniforms beneath, we grabbed handfuls of dirt and lobbed them at one another. Diane was laughing so hard, she started to hiccup, which made us laugh even harder. At last, we managed to stop laughing and lay on our backs, wondering what to do next. But, before we could decide, we heard a frightening shriek.

"Diana, Alexandra Ariana Giannopoulos! What on earth do you think you are doing?"

Diane shot up like a singed cat and tried to brush the dirt from her clothes and the hair from her face. Mrs. Giannopoulos then looked at the knife, which was still stuck into the ground as if into a corpse. Horrified, she grabbed the red silk of her bath robe at the neck as if I were about to plunge the knife into her chest. "It's time you went home," she hissed in a thin, steely voice, which my mum could never emulate, even on one of her worst days. "Diana, come into the house ... now!" With a toss of her beautiful head, Mrs. Giannopoulos marched back into the house, a blister of red rage.

We stood up and helped one another remove the fairy princess dresses and the dirt as best we could.

"I'm sorry, Diane," I muttered as I handed her the hair ribbon.

"I think it might be best if you slipped out the side gate," whispered Diane. "It'll be safer that way! Come to the front door and I'll bring your satchel."

I agreed this was a good idea, and as I made my way back to the front of the house, I stooped beneath the level of the hedge as a precautionary measure. After some time, Diane appeared; I noticed the hair ribbon was back in place. I took my satchel and turned to go, but Diane touched my arm, "I had a good time!" she said, and then as an after thought she added, "Perhaps, next time I could come to your house."

I looked at her. "That's a good idea," I agreed ... but we both knew it could never happen. "See ya," I said.

"See ya."

As I started off down the road, I threw the satchel over my shoulder, which seemed heavier than I remembered, but I waited until I had put some distance between me and Mrs. Giannopoulos before I fumbled with the buckles. When I looked inside, I saw that Diane had filled it to the brim with Kit-Kat bars. I was impressed! *Now that's what I call a real friend*, I thought to myself as I tore ravenously into the first bar. Then, munching happily I set my face toward the north, which was, after all, where I belonged.

Gone Fishing

ONE RARE, SUN DRENCHED SUMMER in the memory of childhood, the school holidays arrived with a promise of fish the size of *lorries*[4]. Rumor had it that Barky Brook was running dry and fish were just lying in the muddy water ripe for the picking. So, the first day we planned a bike ride to the brook to see for ourselves. In case the rumors were true, we took buckets to accommodate the size of the fish. At the time, we were ten and eleven years old and usually we fished with small nets we made out of old stockings—we kept our fish in jam jars where they eventually died. Visions of big fish made us greedy, and we harbored no other thought than to capture as many as we could.

Early in the morning, we set off—there was Clueless, long and skinny, buck-toothed and amiable; Dez, dangerous

4. Trucks

and carrying within him the anger that would later explode into a criminal record; Needy Nealey, red-haired, freckle-faced and lost; Snot—juicy, green and forgiven; and Currant, whose last name was Bun. For some reason long since forgotten, they called me Boz—I was the only girl in their gang because I could beat them all at marbles.

We headed towards the iron train bridge, tin buckets hanging on our handlebars, announcing our mission in a volley of clangs. We pumped uphill to the bridge, muscles roaring their protestations in slicing pains that we ignored. Then, down the other side, we released our agony in whooping cries that were devoured by the roaring wind. Down, down, down, our eyes blinded by tears, we hurtled toward Potter's farm where danger lurked. Our whooping cries became a taunting chant, "Black bugger, black bugger!"

Flying on mechanical birds, we were flung by gravity into harm's way. In a torrent of snarls, Blackie, Potter's vicious little terrier, shot out from the farmyard all bristling hair and flashing teeth.

"Black bugger, black bugger!" we continued our chant, and then in a single choreographed movement, we lifted our feet from the pedals and raised our legs up and out into wings that carried us above the teeth, the hair, and the rage.

We were clear to the other side and beyond when a cry rang out, "Ahhhh, you black bugger!" The flashing teeth had caught the cuff of Snot's trousers. Blackie's body streamed out from Snot's leg, a perpendicular streak of fury. Leaning at a dangerous angle, Snot attempted to compensate for the weight of the dog, which hung on despite being beaten again and again by the demented swinging of the bucket. Dez, who was in the lead, whipped around and drew alongside the dog. With a deft kick he caught Blackie on the rump. Yelping, the dog released its grip and sailed into the air before landing in a dusty heap on its back.

"Black bugger, black bugger," we laughed as we sped off in a noisy din of heartless triumph.

At a more leisurely pace, we spread out—lords of the road—careless of our safety and oblivious to the rights of motorists. When we crested Cricketer's Hill, once more we formed a single line and with heads bent forward we flew like projected missiles from cricketers' bats down the steep incline. Rounding the corner at the bottom, we shot into the intersection causing an egg lorry to swerve dangerously. Its honking horn hailed our arrival in Barkby where the brook, fat with fish, awaited.

Eventually, we left the meandering main road that wound its way through the village and followed the dirt trail by Turpin's farm which led to the brook. Here we abandoned our bicycles and, grabbing the handles of our buckets, clambered toward the bush-tangled banks where we discovered that the brook was dry. All that remained was a long smear of cracked mud.

"We're too late," murmured Currant.

"Don't be daft," spat Dez. "We need to go to the deepest part of the brook to find the fish. That's where they'll be."

"Under the bridge!" yelled Currant.

"To the bridge! To the bridge!" we all yelled dramatically.

"Shhsssh!" warned Dez—as if we were engaged in some sort of illicit activity.

As we struggled along the dry streambed in silence, every now and then the cracked surface gave way and our feet disappeared into the foul-smelling mud beneath. Whenever this happened, Dez sniggered.

Soon, a rank odor of sweet slime and rotting fish filled our nostrils—perhaps we were too late, but no one dared say anything. Dez led the way and as we rounded the corner, we heard him utter a low, sibilant sound. The old bridge, cracked and dried out in the merciless heat, arched above the disaster below as if lifting its brick skirt above the rotting filth that lurked beneath. Dez edged closer, stepping carefully on the green, slippery rocks and disappeared into the fetid gloom under the bridge.

Carefully, we edged along by the wall, which was still slimy and damp in places, until we came to the middle where the water used to be deepest—where in summers past we used to swim, where in summers past we took an old tin bath tub and sailed it like a boat out of the darkness and down the shallow rapids of the brook. We didn't know back then what size of creatures lurked beneath, but here they were stranded as we had hoped. To us they seemed huge—the biggest catfish we'd ever seen. They were be-whiskered and bewildered, flopping and gasping in mud they had once called friend.

"We'll need water," hissed Dez.

"Turpin's farm," Clueless reminded us in a whisper. "There's a tap inside the yard."

It didn't take us long to fill our buckets and return, eager to begin our plunder.

The first to begin, Dez grabbed the biggest fish with both hands and hoisted it high into the air as though at last he had found himself the victor at the end of a long and honorable struggle. Dressed in its armor of mud, the black fish opened and closed it great gaping mouth in silent shouts of protest. Dez plopped it into his bucket where it performed a series of pirouettes before coiling around and around in a desperate attempt to keep its whiskery head submerged.

And then with animal cries that Dez didn't attempt to silence, we fell to looting and pillaging. Clueless got a grand-daddy he reckoned was at least a foot long, a gross exaggeration, but still bigger than anything we'd ever caught before. Needy managed to find two decent sized six-inchers, I snagged a beauty of about eight inches, and we all laughed at Snot who ended up with a tiddler no more than four inches long.

Laughing and slipping, muddied and smelly, we carried our plunder heedless of the water that leaped from our buckets onto the parched ground. When we reached our bicycles, we hung the buckets onto the handlebars. The logistics of riding our bicycles with such heavy buckets had not occurred to us until then, but it didn't take us long to find a solution. If we pointed our knees outward and leaned a little to one side, we could manage to pedal and clear the hanging buckets which banged rhythmically against the metal frames of our bikes. In single file, we made our tortuous way along the dirt path by Turpin's Farm and onto the long country road that wound through the village.

When we came to Cricketer's Hill our spirits and strength gave out. We stopped trying to pedal our over-laden bicycles, and instead we got off and pushed them while our buckets swung back and forth creating small tidal waves that splashed a steaming trail down the dusty road. It was mid-day and the sun beat down mercilessly upon our exposed heads. Currant was sweating profusely and his face had turned beyond bright red to puce. As Clueless pushed his bicycle upwards, he leaned forward so much his skinny body formed a parallel line with the road.

"I can't go on," gasped Needy, and groaning loudly, we all agreed.

Dez glared at us menacingly, "Stop complaining, you bloody weaklings, or I'll give you something to complain about."

We never knew what would set Dez off but after exchanging fearful looks, we plodded on without another word. With boiling faces and straining muscles, we forced our way upwards. When at last we reached the top, we took shelter under an ancient oak that spread its branches between

us and the sky. We removed the buckets from the handlebars
and placed them in the shade. Groaning and gasping, we fell
onto the dry, scorched grass.

We were done for. Going on with our plunder seemed
an impossible feat. Returning with it to the brook was a hurdle
too enormous to contemplate.

"Me throat's parched," gasped Currant. "I could grab
one of them buckets right now and drink the lot."

"That's disgusting," said Snot, but he convinced nobody.
"I could just go for a swig of Dandelion and Burdock pop or a
long gulp of Vimpto," he continued in a tantalizing manner.
We all groaned as visions of long, cool drinks of something,
anything, filled our heads.

"We could get home a whole lot faster without these
bloody fish," suggested Dez.

Immediately, the idea leaped from one to the other like
a mirage in the arid deserts of our brains.

"What'll we do with 'em?" asked Currant.

A moment of silence descended as we considered our
options. Eventually, Needy spoke up. "They'd die at home
eventually, and we couldn't flush these buggers down the
lav', they're too bloody big." Death was the fate of all the fish
we caught; there was nothing in the history of our fishing to
suggest that these would fare any better. However, the diffi-
culty of disposing of what would be monstrous, black corpses
was another thing we hadn't thought about.

In a quiet voice Clueless whispered, "They'd stand

a better chance back at the brook." Everyone groaned in horror, but I knew it was what we should do—we all knew it was what we *ought* to do. The chance to do the right thing yawned before us. I knew that if just one of us could find the courage to speak up, then we all would. But no one moved; no one spoke and just like that the opportunity passed.

Dez smiled and in an oily voice said, "They were going to die back at the brook anyway. They might just as well die here! I tell you what, we'll leave 'em in the buckets, give 'em a bit more time."

"My old man will kill me if I lose this bucket," whimpered Needy in such a pathetic way we all let out a snort of laughter.

"Your old man will kill you anyway," said Dez but he, too, started to laugh. And just like that the tension eased.

United by laughter, we set about our task. We headed toward the deep, shady ditch where we lined up the buckets. To prevent the water from evaporating too quickly, we covered them loosely with branches and leaves. The black, coiled fish lay still—as if slowly absorbing their fate and our treachery.

With a final glance toward our handiwork, Dez retorted, "We've done them a favor really. At least they've got water, which is more than they had before."

"It's more that we've got," added Needy despondently.

We all nodded our agreement, and we actually began to feel sorry for ourselves.

Then, we retrieved our bicycles and climbed onto them.

Without our heavy burdens, we discovered fresh reserves of energy and sped off down the road. And just like that, we left. We had exploited the weak and abandoned the vulnerable. With no more thought for our victims, we turned our backs upon them. Like seasoned politicians, we had cloaked our crimes with the rhetoric of the just. On our way home, our heads filling with tantalizing images of glasses filled with Dandelion and Burdock or Vimpto®, we carelessly made our plans for the next day's adventure.

Aunty Lily

MY AUNTY LILY WAS BEAUTIFUL. She was tall and elegant and always wore her long auburn hair piled high on the top of her head in a bun. She always wore designer clothes and long golden earrings that reached all the way to her shoulders. But the thing I loved best about Aunty Lily was the fact that she swore. She swore like a trooper. She even swore when she came over for tea on Sundays. My mother, who, as a rule, could not abide bad language of any kind, never said a word!

There was an air of mystery surrounding Aunty Lily that I found both compelling and dangerous, and how it was that mother managed to persuade her to take me into town for a much needed pair of school shoes, I'll never know, but such was the case. We set off early one Saturday morning. I was feeling rather dowdy in my homemade cotton dress, but Aunty Lily looked frightening in her little black suit with the nipped-in waist, black silk stockings with seams as straight as two ruled lines, and long, gold gypsy earrings that bounced on her shoulders as she walked.

We walked all the way to the bus stop. We didn't have long to wait. Soon, the Midland Red bus came roaring down the street. It took one look at Aunty Lily and screeched to a halt. The bus driver gaped, the passengers stared, and the young bus conductor tip-toed back from the doorway as if Aphrodite in all her naked glory was standing at the bus stop. Aunty Lily noticed none of this and with an air of unconscious superiority began to board the bus. She was just about to pull herself up when the elastic in her one hundred per cent French Parisian silk camisole knickers broke. Her underwear fluttered around her legs like a flag in a breeze, falling with a silken sigh around her ankles. Everybody froze. There was no movement except for the violent blush that exploded in the lard-pale face of the young conductor.

"Ooooooo ya bugger!" Aunty Lily swore. "Me bloody elastic's broke." Without missing a beat, she stepped out of the offending underwear, shook them, and then folded them before popping them into her purse. A gasp of unabashed admiration rippled among the passengers as we took our seats.

When we got to the bus station, we were allowed to get off the bus first. Without even a backward glance, we sailed into town. We walked all the way through the market place, all the way to a tiny, exclusive shoe shop where my mother only ever dared window shop. We marched right in, and Aunty Lily bought me a pair of black, patent leather, silver buckled, totally unsuitable—I'll never be allowed in town with Aunty Lily again—school shoes. As we came out of the store, I clasped the shoes to my chest and followed Aunty Lily through the market and down the street toward the bus station. All of a sudden, it began to rain. It came down in buckets.

"Sod it!" Aunty Lily swore. "I don't have me bloody umbrella. Come on, Jen!" She grabbed hold of my hand and we ran down the street, all the way to the bus station. We dived into the ladies' lavatory.

She took one look at herself in the mirror and exclaimed, "Ooo ya bugger! I'm bloody well wet through!"

Then, I watched while she set about repairing the damage. First, she spread a little lace handkerchief on the shelf. Then she unpinned the bun from the top of her head—she took it off, dried it, and put it on the shelf. Next, she took out her teeth. She rinsed them in cold water, dried them, and put them next to the bun. Then, for her 'piece de resistance,' she took out her left eye, washed it off and dried it, and placed it next to the teeth.

The transformation was nothing short of miraculous. In a few swift strokes Aunty Lily had changed from a tall elegant woman into a straggle-haired, sunken faced, one eyed old hag. I stared at her in open-mouthed admiration.

She turned and looked at me with her one good eye, "You must always remember this, Jen!"

"I think I will, Aunty."

"No, not this," she said indicating the various parts of her on the shelf. "What I'm about to tell you. Things are never what they seem. Beauty—it's not even skin deep. And always take good care of your teeth!"

"I will, Aunty."

Then, I watched while she put herself back together. She pinned the bun back into position on the top of her head. She opened her mouth and popped her teeth back into place. Then, she carefully inserted the glass eye into the empty eye socket. A little eye shadow, a little lipstick completed the reformation. With a sigh of satisfaction, Aunty Lily stood back from the mirror. "How do I look, Jen?"

Well, I looked at her, and I could see that the auburn of the bun didn't quite match the auburn of her hair. I could see the rigid perfection of the false teeth and the frozen unseeing stare of the glass eye. Suddenly, I realized I was actually seeing Aunty Lily for the very first time, and in that moment, I understood exactly what she had been trying to tell me. Without any further hesitation, I looked at her and said, *"You are beautiful."* And she was!

The Revenge of Stuart Smith

STUART SMITH WAS ODD. He certainly looked odd. He had large, luminous green eyes, a loose sloppy grin and great, big ears, which stuck straight out from his head and were so paper-thin you could see the network of tiny blue veins beneath the skin. He flitted in and out among us like some alien moth, but the strangest thing about him was his silence—he never spoke. He *could* speak, but he just chose not to. We had been friends for as long as I could remember. In all that time, I heard him speak real words only one time.

It was the end of fall and we were coming up to *winter warmer* season. In the rest of the world, time is measured by the passing of the seasons, but on Charnwood Avenue time was measured by the games that we children played. In the spring it was time for whip-and-top, in summer it was stilts and marbles, in the fall it was conkers and snobs, and in winter—why this was the best of all for this was winter warmer season. Stuart and I were eleven years old, and this was the first year we were allowed to make a winter warmer. We went to our respective homes to begin work.

The first thing I needed was an empty tin can. I sneaked into the kitchen and searched through the cupboards until I found what I was looking for—a tin of powdered milk from the welfare, which still contained some dried milk. Making sure my mother was no where in sight, I started to pour it into the trash, but the eyes in the back of her head must have been on high alert. "There are children starving in this world," she declared, stealing up behind me so quietly I almost dropped the tin in fright. "And here you are wasting good food," she concluded pointedly.

I shuffled toward the back door. "Sorry, Mam," I called over my shoulder and escaped to the wash house where I found a hammer and a big nail and started to punch holes in the sides of the tin. This was the tricky part because if you hit the nail too hard, you could put a big dent in the side and the tin would be ruined, so I took my time and worked carefully. Soon the tin was littered with holes. Then I got a long piece of wire and attached it through two holes near the top on either side of the tin to make a handle. I crumpled some newspaper in the bottom and covered it with little bits of wood. I was about to sprinkle some coal on the top when I realized I'd forgotten the most important part and had to sneak back to the kitchen to get it. I didn't relish the thought because I knew I'd be in for the rest of the lecture on the starving masses. Instead, as I tip-toed into the kitchen, there was my mother with a big grin on her face and a freshly washed potato in her hand. "Be careful!" was all she said as she dropped the potato into my winter warmer. It didn't take me long to cover the potato with coal, and then later in the evening I ran next door to call for Stuart. It had just rained and everything smelled fresh and clean like the newly washed potato my mother had given me.

Stuart was already waiting for me at his garden gate. We gave each other's winter warmer the once over and nodded our approval. Smiling, we ran down the darkening, shiny street. We met the other kids in the cul-de-sac, which we called *the ring*, where we played tin-tin-ta-lurky and pie-crust-coming as a way of passing the time until the real purpose of the evening arrived.

When it was good and dark, we retrieved our *winter warmers*. Some were shiny and new, while others were last year's model and were charred black. Then, we gathered in the circle of light under the street lamp. A hushed silence descended and our excitement charged the air like an electric current. We felt as if we were gathered at a sacred altar, taking part in some ancient ritual. I stood next to Stuart and I could feel him shaking.

"Who's got the matches?" whispered Needy. There was a faint rustling and Clueless produced a box and lit a match. In its flare, I could see Dez Scriggin's cruel face with its cold black eyes glittering like beads. The altar that Dez saw was different from ours; his was in need of a sacrifice, animal or human it didn't matter to him. His eyes flickered over each one of us until they came to rest briefly on Stuart. I suppressed a shudder. Dez had always been mean, and he wasn't improving with age. I no longer liked him hanging round with us, not many of us did, but our fear made us silent and accepting.

I dragged my eyes away from his humorless smile and watched as Clueless ceremoniously inserted the lit match into a hole at the bottom of each winter warmer—no religious act was performed with greater reverence. When they were all alight, we grabbed the wire handles and gradually the blackness of the night swallowed us one by one. We spread out down the entire length of the street and simultaneously swung the winter warmers around and around, like you do a bucket of water so that none of it falls out. You could hear the whoosh and roar as each small furnace burst into flame, and you could hear Stuart. Tiny, high-pitched sounds came out of him like an animal's in the night. Not that you could blame him, because when you looked down the street, bright circles of flame sprang in the night, shimmering and roaring like a great fire-breathing dragon.

All too soon, it seemed the mighty dragon died and we gathered once more under the street lamp. We talked in hushed whispers and warmed our hands over the smoldering coals. Just before the fires went out, we shook out our steaming, hot potatoes, sprinkled them with the salt we carried wrapped in a bit of paper in our pockets, and sat and ate in a communal silence.

It wasn't long after that things started to change. Some of the lads started to hang around exclusively with Dez. At first, they started to pick on the little kids but when they got fed up with them, they started picking on Stuart, who was another easy target.

One day after school, I hunted for Stuart to see if he wanted to play but couldn't find him anywhere. In desperation, I even went to his house. Everyone avoided going to Stuart's house because his mam seemed physically incapable of regular, ordinary speech. She screeched, a fingernail-on-the-blackboard-screech, which went right through you.

"I'm not expecting him back 'til bloomin' teatime," she shrieked when I asked for Stuart. I turned on my heel, escaping before she could engage me in a lengthy conversation. I made it to the curb, sat down, and practiced French flydobs with my snobs. Clueless sauntered past. "Hey, Clueless," I yelled, "have you seen Stuart?"

"Stuart?" he asked as if he'd never heard of him before. He looked nervous, and I knew something was wrong.

"What's going on, Clueless?" I grabbed him by his shirt and shook him. He was bigger than me and in a fight he always won, but the victory didn't come easily. I fought like a fox terrier never letting go until someone pulled me off. Clueless, who obviously wasn't in the mood, looked around nervously. "Don't tell anyone I told you or I'll clobber ya. I saw Dez and his lads a little while ago. They were marching Stuart toward the spinney." The spinney was a wooded area at the top of the street. There in a field beyond the trees, Ernie Miller kept his bull.

"Thanks, Clueless," I let him go. "I don't suppose you want to go with me to find him?"

"Are you nuts?" he snorted and shuffled off.

I knew better than to go after Dez by myself, but I knew none of the other kids would dare go with me. So, I had no choice but to use my big guns. I ran down the garden path and dived into the kitchen. "Come quick, Mam. Dez and the lads have got Stuart." Without saying a word, she shot up and started taking off her apron. No law abiding, respectable housewife on Charnwood Avenue would be caught dead in the street wearing an apron—not even, it would seem, to rescue a desperate child. Running up the street, I led the way with the heavy artillery bringing up the rear. I dived into the spinney with my mother surprisingly close on my heels. We ran through the wood yelling Stuart's name until at length we came into the clearing where a big oak stood. There was no sign of Dez or the lads, but Stuart was there. They had tied him to the tree. He was a sorry bedraggled mess. Goodness only knows what they had done to him before we arrived, but as we got closer, it was obvious from the smell that they had peed on him.

"The dirty little buggers!" Mother swore. I was shocked.

I'd never heard my mother swear before, but I could tell by the look in her eye and the set of her jaw that it hadn't just slipped out. It was then that I learned one of life's valuable lessons: sometimes a swear word is not only acceptable but absolutely necessary.

I looked at Stuart. It was the first time I'd ever seen him when he didn't have a smile on his face. His ears drooped, but his eyes were the worst—for the light had gone out. They were red-rimmed, dull, and they were empty.

"Come on my little chicken," crooned Mam as we undid the rope. The heavy artillery melted into marshmallows and we took him home.

I didn't see much of Stuart after that. Whenever I called for him, his mam said he didn't want to play. Instead, I started hanging around with Clueless, who wasn't a bad sort, but every now and then I'd still try Stuart.

One Saturday evening just as it started to get dark, I went to call for Stuart, but I was too late. He was already at the top of the street, swinging a shopping bag back and forth. He must have been on his way to the small grocery store that stayed open a little later on Saturday nights. I yelled his name, but he ignored me. Running after him, I yelled even louder. I knew he had heard me but he just took off running and disappeared round the corner, so I gave up. Oh, I know I should have tried harder, but I knew what he was up to—he thought if he stayed away from me, Dez and the lads would leave me alone.

Not having anything better to do, I went to call for Clueless instead. We roller skated for a while and then we decided to go to the spinney to Ernie Miller's field and do a bit of bull baiting. This activity, of which I'm not particularly proud, involved tormenting the bull by pulling faces, blowing raspberries, and flicking little lumps of clay in its direction until it rolled its eyes and steam poured out from both nostrils. Ernie kept his bull in a barn which had a small circular paddock in front where "Killer" could graze. We called the bull Killer because whenever we saw Ernie, he limped over to us and showed us the horrible scars where the bull had gored him one time. "You keep away from that thar' bull," he'd say, "it be a killer that one." And although we laughed, we always did our bull baiting behind the sturdy fence.

Clueless and I had just reached the end of the spinney when we heard voices coming from Ernie's field. We ducked behind some low bushes and peeked out. We could see Dez and Danny Lagdon, Malcolm Mobbs, Benny Toon, and Walter Babcock. Dez had Stuart under his arms and Walter held his feet and they were swinging him backwards and forwards like a sack of old potatoes. Stuart clutched his shopping bag and its contents as if it were a life preserver and they were about to throw him into deep water. Suddenly, they all began to count in high, sing-song voices and on three Dez and Walter let him go. Stuart flew over the fence, legs flailing, but still clutching the life preserver desperately to his chest.

He landed with a sickening thud in front of the bull. Already wound up, the bull stood wild-eyed with its sides heaving.

Instantly, I leaped to my feet. "Ya' bloody, great big bullies!" I knew instinctively that this was just the right time for a swear word! Clueless grabbed me, pulling me back behind the bushes, but it was too late. Dez had seen us.

"Get 'em lads!" With a single "whoop" they charged after us, and we set off running blindly through the spinney.

"We've got to save Stuart!" I screamed.

"Not me!" yelled Clueless.

"Split up and double back."

"They'll kill us," moaned Clueless. But he did it! I leaped off to the right and Clueless to the left.

"After 'em," yelled Dez. "Don't lose 'em."

It took only a moment for them to split up, but it gave us the edge we needed. Following a semi-circular path through the trees, within seconds of one another we came crashing from the trees into the field. Clueless reached the fence just before me and threw his body against it. Then he froze. I forced myself to look where he was staring, and what I saw made me gasp in horror. Although it was getting dark and a thick mist was drifting upward from the grass, we could still see the bull in the middle of the paddock, pawing the ground angrily. We could see two shoes and though they were mangled and torn and covered with what looked like thick, red blood, we could tell they were Stuart's. Scattered all around were slices of white bread—as if they were trying desperately to mop up the blood. Discarded, the shopping bag lay in an empty, deflated heap. I looked behind the bull into the misty shadows of the dark field beyond to see if I could see Stuart's crushed, lifeless body, but it was getting too dark.

Howling and screaming like a pack of wild animals, Dez and the lads thundered out of the spinney, stopping dead in their tracks when they saw our rigid bodies. Walter was the first to see over the fence. "Oh my God!" he exclaimed. "Do you think the bull's killed him?" Someone laughed a high pitched, nervous laugh and then silence descended while the horror of what had happened sank in. Even Dez was shaken. His face was a deathly white, and the glass beads of his eyes were like holes in his head. Time slowed down. Everything was in slow motion as if we were under water. Then something made Dez look toward the barn. Slowly, his mouth dropped open and what little blood was left drained from his face. We followed his gaze. To our dismay, we saw something hanging in mid-air in the misty darkness beside the door. The lamp above the door of the barn shed enough watery light to show that it was a human form but its legs and feet had been devoured by the mist. The eerie light cast dark shadows over its face making its eyes look like two empty sockets. Its mouth hung open in a large gaping hole and its ears stuck straight out from its head like two transparent wings.

"It's Stuart," Malcolm whispered. "He's come to haunt us."

No one moved. Time had stopped and was holding us relentlessly in its grasp. Slowly and deliberately, the ghost—or whatever it was—lifted its long, skinny arm and pointed its bony finger at Dez. Time released the rest of us long enough for us to take one step away from him. Then the apparition began to screech in a loud, terrible voice. "If you prick us, do we not bleed? If you tickle us, do we not laugh? If you poison us, do we not die? And if you wrong us, do we not REVENGE?" The terrible voice was like ten fingernails scraping down a board. Even Killer scampered over to the far side of the paddock in an attempt to escape the terrible sound. Suddenly, time sped up and unleashed everyone. We exploded into a run, screaming and tripping over one another in an effort to escape. Gripped by terror, we crashed out of the spinney into the safety of the street beyond, where I bent double to recover from the stitch which stabbed me in the side like a knife. Straightening at last, I watched the others as they poured down the street in a deluge of panic until they disappeared into the safety of their respective homes. Suddenly, in that moment, everything fell into place.

Once I recovered my breath, I ran back through the spinney, into the field, and around to the far side of the barn where it connected with the paddock fence. On top, I could see Stuart standing in his stocking feet.

"Ha! Ha! You were brilliant!" I laughed, but of course, Stuart didn't say anything—he just grinned.

"Come on," I shouted. Infused with a reckless courage,

we ignored the bull and climbed over the fence to retrieve Stuart's shoes and empty shopping bag. We cleaned them off as best we could before setting off for my house to replace the lost bottle of ketchup and the loaf of bread he had bought earlier. The shop was closed now and Stuart's mother would kill him if he went home without them.

As we walked down the deserted street, we didn't say another word. There was no need. Stuart just smiled, his mouth hung open in a loose, sloppy grin, his eyes, which were the vivid, vibrant green they had always been, shone is the darkness, and his ears stuck straight out from his head like two transparent wings. Once more we felt the old, comfortable silence settle around us—a silence as golden and precious as our friendship.

The Arrival

WHEN GRANDDAD CAME TO LIVE WITH US, he arrived in bits and pieces. For many weeks my father had been bringing Granddad's possessions and installing them in the front room, which was to be his bedroom and sitting room. However, Granddad insisted on making the final journey himself.

It was this insistence that prompted my mother to call a family council meeting. Now, the term council meeting conjures images of lively debate and the free flowing exchange of ideas, but nothing could have been further from the truth. We four children sat around the kitchen table stony-faced and silent while Mother told us in no uncertain terms what was expected of us. Our involvement was simple: show up, sit up, and shut up.

On this particular occasion, Mother wanted to impress upon us the need to make Granddad feel at home and above all to make him feel useful.

"Do you all understand?" she asked in a quiet, urgent voice, "Under no circumstances must Granddad feel that he has lost his independence." She said the word "independence" as if it were a secret password written on a piece of paper that we must chew and swallow. We nodded our heads solemnly and, without having uttered a single word, another family council was satisfactorily concluded.

The very next morning, John, the youngest member of our family, and I set off to the bus stop to await Granddad's arrival.

"Granddad could be on any bus," yelled Mother. "You could be waiting all day!"

"That's all right, Mum. We don't mind." Not knowing which bus he was on allowed us to ride the waves of anticipation that gathered with the arrival of each Midland Red bus. Six buses came and went and six times the excitement built to an unbearable peak only to topple and crash in a sea of disappointment.

With the arrival of the seventh bus, the bus conductor, on seeing our crestfallen faces, wanted to know who we were waiting for.

"Our Granddad's coming to live with us," I informed him.

"He's very old," John added, as if this somehow explained why Granddad had not yet appeared.

The bus conductor took this as a professional affront, as

if the Midland Red Bus Company was somehow responsible for the loss. "Don't worry," he assured us. "I'm sure he'll be on the next run."

I didn't like to inform him that Granddad was neither late nor lost, and that we had no idea when he was likely to arrive. However, seeing the bus roar off with the conductor hanging out of the door yelling, "The Midland Red always gets its man!" added to our excitement and filled us with the comforting sense that the bus company was out to hunt Granddad down not merely transport him.

And get him it did! On the very next run when the bus turned the corner at the bottom of the street, we saw the bus conductor hanging out of the door, yelling above the roar of the engine, "Mission accomplished! Mission accomplished!" The bus screeched to a halt and the bus conductor stood back from the doorway as Granddad appeared.

"Tadaaaaaaa!" the bus conductor cried, like a magician who had made a rabbit magically appear out of a hat.

"Oh, thank you," I cried.

"Don't mention it. All in a day's work." He handed Granddad his suitcase. Granddad, not surprisingly, was looking rather confused by all of this, and then the bus roared off in a triumphant puff of smoke.

John, who had been beaming mightily up to this point, stopped smiling. "What's up, Granddad?" he asked

Granddad was looking troubled and was systematically patting his breast and hip pockets, as if he had lost something very important.

John's fat face creased with concern, and he whispered ferociously to me, "I think he's lost his independence."

"Shhssss!" I admonished him, "Granddad will hear you!"

Granddad glared at us. "I've lost my bloomin' hat!" He continued to pat him pockets, though it was quite obvious to us that they could hardly conceal a large, felt trilby hat. Just then, the bus came roaring back down the street and stopped across from where we were standing. The bus conductor jumped off and ran over to us.

"Here you are, Governor," he said and handed Granddad his hat. "You take good care of your granddad," he shouted to us as he swung back on to the bus.

I remembered Mother's directives from the night before, and I said, more sharply than I intended, "Our Granddad can take care of himself!"

Granddad looked a little taken aback, but then his face eased into a smile. "I could do with a nice cup of tea," he said. I was about to pick up the suitcase, but then I thought better of it. The word "independence" rang in my head like an alarm.

"Right oh, Granddad." John and I skipped down the street as Granddad struggled valiantly with his suitcase. We opened the gate for him and Mother came rushing out of the house. She hugged Granddad, and then looked crossly at the suitcase in his hand. "Eh, up, Dad, they never let you carry your own suitcase!" She took it from him and placed it on the ground before us. "What kind of children are you?"

I was about to explain about independence and feeling useful, but the tight, thin-lipped expression on her face warned me against it. Pointing to the suitcase, she said, "Put that in Granddad's room—and no ifs, ands, or buts." Then, she led him into the kitchen where he could rest while she made him his cup of tea.

With a great sigh, I looked down at John—his plump, red cheeks were scrunched up so that his eyes were lost in a nest of lines. He was a study of confusion and incredulity. With a great sigh, I said to him, "John, when you get to my age, nothing an adult says or does will make any sense whatsoever." And then with a weariness beyond my years, I stooped to pick up the suitcase, knowing that understanding the difference between dependence and independence would be as difficult as understanding the difference between being told I'm taking too much apple crumble and me thinking it's not enough!

The Adventure

WHEN GRANDDAD CAME TO LIVE WITH US, we knew our lives would never be quite the same again. He made his presence felt almost immediately. As soon as we had installed the last of his belongings in the front room, which was to be Granddad's living room and bedroom, we gathered around the kitchen table to have our tea.

Granddad eyed us critically and turned to father and said, "Albert! These children have pasty faces!"

"They do!" agreed my father.

"What they need is some vigorous exercise!"

"They do!" agreed my father, who was a man of few if treacherous words.

"Right, I'll take them on a good long walk tomorrow."

We could tell by the look in Granddad's eye that argument was futile and our fate was sealed.

The next morning I woke up bright and early. I needed to go to the lavatory, but I think it was more the excitement of knowing Granddad was in the front room that made me wake at such an ungodly hour. As I passed by the front room, I noticed that Granddad's door was open, and I peeked in to see if he was awake. I got a bit of a shock because in the bed was a head and a pair of feet. He was so skinny that in between—where his body should have been—the bed clothes were perfectly flat. More surprising than this was the missing walrus mustache. Granddad had a beautiful white mustache of which he was inordinately proud. Now his head was thrown back, his mouth was wide open and the beautiful, walrus mustache had disappeared.

While I was pondering this mystery, a great exhalation of breath burst forth from Granddad's mouth accompanied by a low deep moan not unlike the noise a seal makes, "Hooonnkkk!" And out with it shot the mustache. It hovered over Granddad's cavernous mouth with its exposed pink gums and then quickly disappeared with the next rapid intake of breath. I watched it re-appear and disappear a number of times before Mother stole up behind me and boxed me on the ears. "Stop being so bloomin' necky!" She firmly closed the door.

"Sorry, Mum!" And I went outside to the lav'. I hurried up. It was freezing cold and filled with spider webs. When I came back in, Granddad was dressed and was having his first cup of tea of the day. I sat by him and we had tea and toast together. I loved watching Granddad eat. He had no teeth and each time he chewed, his face collapsed in the middle throwing nose and chin onto a dangerous collision course.

One by one Richard, Katherine, and John came down for breakfast. When everyone had finished, we set off on the threatened walk. We glided down the garden path and sailed into Charnwood Avenue, a flotilla with Granddad as the figure head looking magnificent in grey felt trilby hat, grey suit, and a blue waistcoat with a gold fob watch in the pocket. He carried an ornately carved walking stick. What had started out as an expedition had turned into an exhibition and Granddad was the main exhibit! We walked up Charnwood Avenue, turned into Highway Road, and went all the way to the train bridge. We thought this was far enough, but it wasn't far enough for Granddad. He said we could watch one train and then we'd be on our way.

We climbed up and poked our heads over the metal side of the bridge. Soon, a train arrived with a thunderous roar, swallowing us in a great cloud of smoke. Our eyes watered and our throats burned but we never let go until the last carriage was beneath us. Then, we yelled, "Jack-in-the-box, Jack-in-the-box!" until the guard appeared and waved to us with his smoked-stained flag. When we jumped down, our faces were speckled with black coal dust—we looked like four escaping desperadoes. Richard let out a bloodcurdling yell and ran off. We set off after him as fast as hares climbing over stiles and crawling under hedgerows. All the time, Granddad plodded behind us with the relentlessness of a tortoise. We must have gone for miles before John and Granddad began to tire. Granddad sat down on an old tree stump. "We'll sit here and rest a while, and then you can show me the way home."

There was a stunned silence. "But we don't know how to get home," said Katherine in a small, frightened voice, and the awful truth dawned on us that we were lost.

We had never been lost with an adult before and it was very disturbing. John started to cry loudly. "Hush now," said Granddad. "It's not as bad as all that!" Granddad, however, had removed his hat and was mopping his brow nervously. When Katherine's lip started to tremble, he rallied to the occasion. "Right oh, Richard. You're the eldest. You look after the little ones and I'll go off and find out where we are."

He set off leaving us feeling quite optimistic until he disappeared over the brow of the hill, and then we sat and waited in a desultory silence, broken occasionally by sniffles from Katherine and heaving sobs from John. We waited an awfully long time. Shadows grew across the field and swallowed us in a chilling gloom.

Suddenly, Richard leapt to his feet. "What's that?" We listened. There was a thin whine which got louder and louder until suddenly it burst into a roar and a tractor came over the hill. It was pulling a hay wagon and sitting on the top bale of hay was Granddad waving his trilby and brandishing his stick. It drew up alongside us. "Climb aboard my hearties," Granddad cried looking positively piratical. "We're traveling home in style."

We clambered aboard and the tractor roared to life, the bales of hay shifting precariously beneath us.

"Hang on," Granddad cried. He was laughing delightedly, his mustache disappearing and reappearing like puffs of smoke from a train. The ride became a little more sedate when we reached the road, but Granddad became more animated and he started to sing, "Rule Britannia, Britannia rules the waves." The farmer joined in. "Britain never, never, never shall be slaves."

As we turned down Highway Road and into Charnwood Avenue, we could see Mother standing at the garden gate waiting anxiously. She looked furious, like mothers do when they're relieved to see their children safe and sound. As we trundled down the street, kids ran out of their houses and skipped behind the hay wagon singing along with the farmer and Granddad. Granddad waved his stick like a campaigning politician and yelled, "The sun never sets on the British Empire!" The tractor rumbled to a halt in font of our house and we jumped off. Mother and the farmer helped Granddad down. She thanked the farmer.

"Oh, that's all right, me duck," he laughed. "I wouldn't have missed it for the bloomin' world." She waited until he was gone before she turned on Granddad. "I thought you were taking them for a walk?"

"A walk, Barbara?" Granddad looked offended. "It wasn't a walk, it was an adventure! An adventure!" The kids cheered as he winked at us and walked down the garden path swinging his stick like Charlie Chaplin.

And for us the adventure continued, but not so for Mother. Granddad's behavior, which had always been erratic even at the best of times, became worse. However, it was his increasing forgetfulness that worried Mother. Granddad loved to do the shopping, but one day he set off and didn't come back for hours and hours. Eventually, he tottered up the street after the Unicorn and Star, a public house of low repute, had closed its doors. He had lost the groceries but had found a large, red faced lady who kissed him shamelessly at the garden gate. On another occasion, he set off with John in his *pushchair*[5]. This time he remembered the groceries but had lost John whom we found a few hours later fast asleep in the alley by the butcher's shop. After that, Mother insisted that one of us children had to go with him to keep an eye on him. Not that we minded, because we never knew what might happen.

One Saturday morning, I had to go with Granddad to the chemist's to get his prescription filled. We walked down Charnwood Avenue, down Redhill lane, and as we turned into Melton Road, we passed by some terraced houses. The front doors came to a point at the top like castle doors and were close together like soldiers in a row. As we walked by, Granddad muttered to himself, "Perfect! Perfect!"

"What is Granddad?"

"You'll see."

---

5. Stroller

We went to the chemist and got his medicine, but when we came out, Granddad slipped into the hardware store before I could stop him. He came out with a clothesline. He chuckled all the way to the terraced houses where he became deadly serious and started peering in at the windows and listening at the *letter boxes*[6].

"Granddad! You'll have us arrested!"

"Eh, up! You're worse than your mother, Jen." The accusation hit home and I found myself peering through Mrs. Smith's keyhole. "Mrs. Smith's home," I whispered.

"Same here. These'll do."

Granddad took out the clothesline and measured off a length and cut it with his penknife. He gave one end to me. "Tie that around the doorknob." I did as I was told while Granddad tied his end to the other door knob. When we finished, the line stretched between the two, neither too tight nor too loose.

"Right! When I count to three, Jen, you knock on that door as loud as you can. Ready? One, two, three!"

I pounded on my door. He pounded on his. Then, he grabbed my arm and dragged me across the street where we could watch without being seen. Mrs. Smith opened her door first. It didn't open very far and as soon as Mrs. Preston opened her door, Mrs. Smith's slammed shut. Mrs. Smith opened her door again, and Mrs. Preston's slammed shut. We watched the doors open and close, open and close until

---

6   Letter slots

Mrs. Smith stuck her foot in the door and yelled, "Eh up, you little monkeys, come and untie this string or I'll give you a bloomin' thick ear!" Of course, no "little monkeys" appeared and the only way for the two women to get to the front doors was to walk along the back of the houses and into the side alley. While they were doing this, Granddad and I slipped into Redhill Lane unseen. We giggled all the way home. We were still laughing as we walked into the kitchen.

"What have you two been up to?" demanded Mother suspiciously.

"Nothing," I said. "Right, Granddad?"

But Granddad wasn't laughing anymore. His eyes were glazed and he looked lost and frightened. "I can't quite remember, Barbara." Then he shuffled off to his room to rest.

Of course, it was all my fault. "See what you've done, Jen. You've overexcited him. It's too much for him."

Mother's concern at last turned into a genuine fear that maybe Granddad's mind was beginning to go. As far as we kids were concerned, there was no doubt about it. We knew his mind was beginning to go and what's more we knew exactly where it was when it went. It slipped from the constraining world of adult reality, slid into the childhood world of his past, and arrived effortlessly into the childhood world of our present. Each slip was an adventure that we hoarded like pirates hoarding stolen treasure. It was like having an accomplice the same age as ourselves, but whose advice had the weight of a whole lifetime's misdemeanors behind it.

I had the dreaded Miss Hacket for geography that year. We called her the Hatchet because she had a sharp, hooked nose and a vicious tongue famous for its verbal lashings. I was determined to play a trick on her for April Fool's Day, but what to do? I decided to consult the expert. Granddad's eyes lit up. He thought for a few moments and then whispered, "Bring me a piece of chalk."

After school, I brought home the chalk. "It's blue Granddad. It' the only piece I could find."

"Let's hope she has to draw a map with lots of rivers."

"We're studying the Amazon," I replied.

"That'll do!" Granddad giggled like the school boy he had become. He took out his penknife and opened up a long, thin attachment and began to bore a hole into the end of the chalk. He worked furiously like a man possessed. Then, he took a box of Blue Swan Matches from his pocket and inserted a match into the hole—the blue of the match blended perfectly with the blue of the chalk. He gave it to me as though it were a stick of dynamite.

The very next day was April Fool's Day. I could hardly wait for geography. At last, fourth period arrived. I walked into the classroom and surreptitiously replaced the blue chalk on the board with my loaded stick and then quickly took my seat, for the Hatchet had arrived. She sliced into the room and eyed us suspiciously before she began the lesson. She went on and on about the Amazon. Almost half the period had gone and she still hadn't drawn the map yet. "Dear God,"

I prayed," please let her draw a map."

At long last, she walked toward the board and picked up the white chalk and drew the outline of South America. My heart was beating so loudly—Boom! Boom! Boom!—I felt sure everyone could hear it. Then, the Hatchet picked up the blue chalk—BOOM! BOOM! BOOM!—and in one, fluid stroke drew the entire length of the Amazon River. Suddenly, there was a horrible crackling sound and the chalk burst into flame. With a scream, she threw it into the air. It flew above our heads like a flare, and when it landed, she jumped on it pounding it into a pile of blue dust. The image of my head under her heel flashed across my mind for just a moment, but I couldn't think about that now, for all the kids were crying: "April fool! April fool!"

I had never seen the Hatchet look so angry. Her eyes were slits, her nose a meat cleaver.

"Who is responsible for this?" Her voice was glacial, freezing the smiles from our faces. "You will all be punished unless the person responsible owns up." The words fell from her mouth like shards of ice.

I had no choice; slowly I raised my hand. "I did."

The Hatchet smiled a thin, blood chilling smile. "Come with me."

I was given three whacks with what was euphemistically called "the slipper," the size twelve gym shoe that was used to dole out punishment to both boys and girls alike. Then, I was sent home in disgrace. The Hatchet's fury paled in comparison to my mother's for no member of the Blount family had ever had the slipper. I had single-handedly lost our unblemished reputation. After I had suffered the full brunt of her anger, I was sent early to bed with no supper. I assumed Granddad had forgotten his part in the crime because he didn't mention it. A few months later, however, he must have had a flashback or something of the sort, because one morning when I took him his tea and toast, he turned to me and demanded, "Well, what happened with the chalk and the Hatchet?"

"Oh, Granddad! I wish you could have been there. The Hatchet was like an avenging angel dousing the flames of hell." At school, Miss Turner had read to us from *The Pilgrim's Progress* and it had made a tremendous impression on me. Suddenly, I became aware of Mother standing at the door with more toast for Granddad. Her lips had disappeared into two straight lines. "I might have known Granddad put you up to that. It's just the sort of juvenile, hare-brained, dangerously stupid thing your Granddad would come up with."

I turned to Granddad expecting his face to be radiant with pride, but it wasn't. His eyes had that glazed, glassy look, and his face was as blank as a plain sheet of paper.

It wasn't long after this that Mother came up with the idea of *draughts*[7]. Draughts, she reasoned wouldn't be too exciting, but would be enough to keep Granddad busy and us out of trouble. Thus began our daily battles over the draught board. Now at first, when Granddad was winning all the time,

7   Checkers

everything was fine. But as I became better at the game and started winning, the situation deteriorated rapidly. Granddad was worse than a spoiled child and couldn't bear to lose.

"Barbara," he shouted one day, "she's cheating!"

"I'm not cheating, Granddad, I'm winning."

"Same thing!" he roared, stomping out of the room and threatening to pack his bags.

Mother came running, wanting to know what the matter was. When I explained, she was most indignant. "You must let him win!" she cried.

This was a revolutionary concept, one that—in the dog-eat-dog world of our neighborhood—I had never contemplated before. Mother coaxed him back to the table, and I started to let him win. If such a thing were possible, Granddad was worse at winning than he was at losing. He crowed and gloated over his victories, howling horribly when I purposely made a mistake. But at long length, after winning constantly, boredom set in. Granddad began to tire of the game. Mother became frantic trying to devise new ways to keep Granddad occupied. Father, in his usual quiet way came up with the solution. "It's not long 'til Christmas," he said. "We'll have a Christmas party."

Granddad had never been so animated. His excitement infected everyone and we all got into the swing of preparation. We helped Mother make sausage rolls, trifles, and mince pies. We boiled hams and Christmas puddings, and we decorated the house with crepe paper streamers. Granddad loved it, but every now and then we found him peering anxiously out of the window. "Just looking for snow," he said, but we all knew he was looking for the red-faced lady so he could invite her.

At last, everything had been baked, brewed, and boiled. The day of the party arrived and at six o'clock the guests began to arrive. They poured in through the door, a never-ending stream of happy humanity. There was Aunty Cis' and Uncle Ted. Aunty Cis' was six feet tall and had a huge bosom like twin mountain peaks. Uncle Ted at five foot four hardly looking the intrepid mountaineer! There was Aunty Lily and Uncle Harry. Aunty Lily was beautiful but she had a glass eye—which was a great tragedy according to my mother, who was of the opinion that three good eyes at the very least were necessary to keep Uncle Harry in line. Then, there was straight-laced Aunty Flo'. She was married to Uncle Jack who loved to tell us dirty stories. There was Uncle Vern' and Aunty Kath. There were friends and relatives, and last, but by no means least, the red-faced lady. She wore purple and looked like a plum!

Mother made sure the guests had something to eat and Father gave everyone a glass of homemade dandelion or elderberry wine. Then, Mother began to play the piano and the "plum" began to sing. Ethel, that was her real name, had a beautiful voice that was as thick and rich as Guinness stout. She began to sing "Ain't she sweet?"

Drooling, Granddad joined in, and in greater detail than my mother thought necessary, pointed out Ethel's finer features to the entire company.

Mother played "Knees up Mother Brown" and skirts were lifted dangerously high to reveal pink knees and white bloomers. The plum wore knee length purple bloomers. We were thrilled. Nice women, we were led to believe, always wore white! Aunty Cis and Uncle Ted started dancing cheek to bosom, Aunty Lily and Uncle Harry were doing a complicated jitterbug, and Aunty Flo' sat thin lipped and tight knee'd, restraining Uncle Jack with a stare.

At last, Mother stopped playing. "Time for trifle. Dad," she said looking around, "will you help me serve the pudding? Dad?" She scanned the room again. "Ethel, have you seen Walter?"

"He went to get his pipe, luv. He's been gone for a long time."

Mother sent us to look for him. Richard and John went upstairs and Katherine and I looked downstairs. We checked in his room first but there was no sign of him or his pipe. We ran into the hallway and noticed that the front door was open. We ran to tell Mother.

"Oh, Al, do you think he's wandered off? He'll catch his death of cold. He doesn't have his hat or his top coat."

"Don't worry," said my father. "He can't be far away." The men threw on their coats and disappeared into the cold night to search the streets. Not knowing what else to do, we children started clearing away the dirty plates while the women made pots of tea, which is the automatic response to any British emergency. They were on their second pot when we heard my father and the men outside. They were laughing. "It's all right, Barbara, we've found him."

Granddad came in the back door and glared at everyone grumpily.

"Oh, Dad," Mother cried, "are you all right?"

"Course I'm all right! Can't an old man go to the lavatory without a search party being launched?"

"The lavatory? But what took you so long?"

"Well, if you must know, when I undid my suspenders, I threw them over my head a bit too hard and they got stuck on a nail up in the rafters. I was hanging there all this time like a sack of old potatoes."

We all began to laugh, which Granddad didn't appreciate at first, but he brightened considerably when Ethel sidled up to him and gave him a wet, noisy kiss on the cheek. Then, she began to sing—quietly at first, "Oh dear, what can the matter be? One old man got stuck in the lavat'ry. He was there from Monday to Saturday. Nobody knew he was there."

Everyone joined in and soon Granddad was laughing and singing along with the rest of us.

The party broke up in the early hours of the morning with Ethel singing "Silent Night" while we ate more of Mother's trifle and mince pies. Ethel became a regular visitor after that, which pleased Mother to no end. Ethel was more than enough to keep Granddad occupied, but he surprised me one day when he asked me if I wanted to play a game of draughts.

"I'd love to, Granddad," I said suddenly realizing how much I had missed playing the game with him. We settled down at the table. He made his move and then he took the pipe out of his mouth and pointed the stem at me. "And no more letting me win!" I was about to argue but he waved his pipe to silence me. "Nobody likes to lose," he said, "but I expect I shall get used to it."

We didn't get to finish the game, however. Halfway through, Granddad's pipe fell out of his mouth. His mouth hung open and was pulled down at one side. I knew what was happening but I didn't rush. I retrieved the pipe, which had fallen between the arm of the chair and Granddad's leg. I didn't want him to get burnt. His pale blue eyes filled with unshed tears and he tried to speak. I knew what he wanted to say. "Just when you were winning fair and square, eh, Granddad?" The good side of his mouth smiled weakly.

Mother came in. I thought she would be angry because I didn't call her right away, but she wasn't. She smiled gently and told me to run to the phone box and call Dr. Whitelaw. The doctor came and made Granddad comfortable. "He's got a couple of days, Missus." The doctor was Irish and believed in simple remedies. "Give him one shot of Irish whiskey twice a day. It'll do him a power of good!"

Just as the doctor predicted, Granddad died two days later. I got up early on that second morning and as I went by Granddad's room, I peeped in. The head was thrown back, his mouth was wide open, and the beautiful white, walrus mustache had disappeared. But I knew no matter how long I waited, there would be no honk and no mustache would come shooting out like a great puff of white smoke.

At the funeral party, we remembered all the things that had happened since Granddad had come to live with us. Father reminded us of the time he had lost us children. Katherine remembered the time he had lost John, Aunty Cis' wiped her eyes remembering the time we had lost him in the lavatory, and Mother proudly recalled how with Granddad's help, I had single-handedly lost our family's unblemished reputation. But all those losses were memories we had won, and each one had been an adventure. We had known when Granddad first came to live with us that our lives would never be quite the same again. It was only now when we had lost him for good that we realized how impoverished our lives would be without him. Slowly absorbing this truth, we said our goodbyes and wished him well as he embarked upon his last adventure, which we hoped would be the greatest adventure of all.

Sundays

SUNDAY AT OUR HOUSE WAS THE MOST MAGICAL day of the week. It was a day filled with rituals lovingly performed week after week until they took on the magnitude of religious observances. It was the only day of the week when Father didn't have to go to work, and it was his presence that created the beat that gave the day its rhythm.

The first ritual began at the crack of dawn when, one by one, we crawled into bed with Mother and Father. There were four of us: Richard, Katherine, myself and John. I have to point out that—at the time—having any children at all was difficult for most English people to understand. Having more than the allotted 2.5 was inconceivable and an indication at the very worst that you demonstrated a total lack of self control or at best you were eccentric. Anyway, the four of us found a niche for ourselves in between, on top, or alongside the warm lumpy bodies of our eccentric parents. This bed was the inner sanctum where we breathed in the wonderful mixture of warm smells, which was the incense, the balm of our existence. After cups of tea and *biscuits*[8], we were evicted from this Garden of Eden so that Mother could have some peace and quiet while Father went downstairs to begin the next ritual of the day.

It was Father's job to cook the breakfast on Sundays. He called it "the works:" eggs, bacon, sausage, tomatoes, and fried bread. When breakfast was ready, he came to the bottom of the stairs and yelled, "Eh up! Grub's up," and we'd all come galloping down to the kitchen table. If the bed was our inner sanctum, this table was our sacred altar. Father sat at the head, and Mother sat at the tail. Just before we started to eat, they looked at one another and smiled. And for a moment time itself was suspended. My parents loved one another passionately and above all things. There was never any doubt in our minds that if the entire family were in a lake drowning, Mother and Father would rescue one another first and then, if we were still alive, they might come back and rescue us. The smile that passed between them, though never directed toward us, was the cornerstone upon which our existence rested. It was our blessing.

After breakfast, father indulged in the third ritual of the day. "Right oh, you lot. I'm about to read the Sunday paper, and I don't expect to be interrupted for any reason, not unless

8 Cookies

of course, you're in the process of choking to death." This was a proviso Father added one Sunday when John actually turned blue in the face before any one of us dared interrupt the sacred ritual of reading the paper.

After the paper had been read, it was time for Katherine and me to go to church. We were the only members of our family who attended a regular church. Father—a raging socialist with definite communist leanings—was of the opinion that organized religion was responsible for many, if not all, the social ills of the world. Mother, on the other hand, was an ardent spiritualist who kept up a continual dialogue with the deceased members of our family every Wednesday night via the medium at the Leicester City Spiritualist Church. So, when it came to deciding whether or where to send their children for spiritual guidance, my parents had a bit of a problem. Father, not entirely opposed to democracy, agreed with Mother that we should be allowed to decide for ourselves, and so it was that one Sunday afternoon we all set off dutifully for the Church of England Sunday School, which was led by Reverend Bottrel. After attending only one time, my brothers agreed with Father that the church was indeed responsible for many social ills, boredom in their opinion being the most unforgivable. Katherine and I were far more dogged than they, and we transferred our allegiance to the local Primitive Bethel Methodist Chapel, which so impressed us with its clamorous singing that we attended three times every Sunday.

If we loved the riotous singing, it was really Miss Taylor's stories that kept us coming back week after week. One particular Sunday, she told the story about an old woman who had a grocery shop, and every Monday morning when Joe, the delivery man, brought the fresh bread, he asked the same question, "Well, what was the sermon about this week, ma' duck?"

And she always answered in the same way. "Oh, you know me, Joe, I can never remember."

Joe laughed, "Waste o' time goin' then ain't it luv?" Eventually, she had enough and one Monday when he asked the same question, she didn't answer. Instead, she reached underneath the counter and took out a dirty, dusty, old basket. "Do me a favor, Joe, and fill this basket with water from the stream outside." Joe scratched his head doubtfully, but he said, "All right ma' duck. I'll try." Of course no matter how many times he tried, the water always leaked out. At length he gave up, came back into the shop, and threw the basket onto the counter in disgust.

The old woman pointed at the basket and said, "That's just what I'm like, Joe. Every Sunday I go to church, but I can't hold the sermon in my head. But just like that old basket when I come home, I'm all clean and fresh!"

Oh, we loved that story. After Sunday school, we ran up the back alley feeling all clean and fresh, dodging the dog turds liberally strewn along the path, singing and believing, "Jesus wants me for a sunbeam to shine for him each day."

When we reached home, we burst into the kitchen, and dived into a sea of sumptuous smells: roast leg of lamb, tangy mint sauce, Yorkshire pudding, and when we surfaced, it was in a hot cloud of potato steam. In the middle, we found mother. "Hello, my little chickens," she cried.

"We're not chickens. We're sunbeams."

"Of course you are! Hungry ones! Sit down. Dinner won't be long."

We sat and watched while she set the table, made the gravy, and drained the vegetables. We never volunteered to help—we weren't expected to. In fact, we never did any chores around the house. We never washed a dish, we never peeled a potato, and we never even made our own beds. "Play is children's work," Mother declared and we believed her! It was a conviction she had held fervently ever since before she was married.

A Romany gypsy came to her house selling lavender, Mother bought some and the gypsy told her fortune. She told Mother that her life would come to an end when she was forty-three. So great was my mother's respect for Romany prophecy that she never doubted the truth of this prediction for one moment. And so, when she married and had us children, she devoted herself to loving her husband and to preserving the magic of our childhood for as long as she was allowed. We never worried about the prophecy, because forty-three meant you were ancient and Mother never ever could be ancient!

After gathering around the altar to enjoy our delicious

Sunday dinner, Father indulged in the most sacred ritual of all: after dinner nap time. He settled down in his easy chair and allowed one of us to stand behind him in the chair so that we could comb his long, silvery gray hair and massage his scalp until he fell into a deep, dreamless sleep. Of course, this meant that we were trapped for the duration of the nap, which—oddly enough—none of us seemed to mind.

The last ritual of the day was observed in the evening when we settled down in front of the television to eat cheese sandwiches with pickled onions, and watch *Sunday Night at the London Palladium*. The variety show always ended in the same way with a circle of sequined, feathered ladies going around and around on a revolving stage, waving goodbye in time to the dreary signature tune. Then, with a click, the television set was turned off. The last magical beat had been played, and there was nothing to look forward to but the bleak despair of Monday morning with its inevitable threat of school.

Thus was the passing of our time measured. We wanted it to go on like this for ever. The only problem with rituals and with the rhythms that sustain them is that they can be so easily disturbed. This disturbance came for us in the form of a Mrs. Whistlebotham, who in our village was the leader of the conservative moral right. She took it upon herself to protect the village from the threat of moral decay she decided my father presented. Her campaign started shortly after Father registered John, the youngest, for school. Whenever Father registered us children for school where it said, "Religious

Affiliation," he conscientiously wrote in the block capitals: I.S.T.S.. Mrs. Peg, who had been registering children for years, was far too sensible to ask any awkward questions. But when Father went to register John, Mrs. Peg had retired and had been replaced by none other than Mrs. Whistlebotham's daughter, who was anything but sensible. "I say, Mr. Blount, is that some obscure branch Islam?"

"No, it bloomin' well isn't! We're Ists! I'm a socialist, my wife's a spiritualist. My two daughters are Methodists, and," he added with a proud flourish, "my two sons are downright anarchists!"

According to Father, it was mention of the two Methodists that pushed Mrs. Whistlebotham over the Church of England edge and forced her to the rescue. At first she just spied on us, which she could do quite easily since her daughter had just moved into the house across the street from us. Every morning when Father left for work, he made sure that Mrs. Whistlebotham was at her post. Next, he grabbed Mother in a passionate embrace and kissed her full on the lips for one minute and thirty seconds. Then, he leaped onto his bicycle yelling, "Be ready to make more babies later, Barbara!"

The situation was obviously worse than Mrs. Whistlebotham had anticipated, and so she began her attacks immediately, posting into our letter box religious leaflets, pamphlets, and booklets in enormous quantities. When these failed to have the desired effect, she decided to get at "the heart of the problem" when "the heart of the problem" was at home. And so on Sundays, on this sacred day of the week, she launched her main attack. This took the form of strategic interruptions which she was able to time with a military precision of which Field Marshal Montgomery himself would have been proud, for they coincided with the most sacred moments in Father's blessed day.

While we were in the "inner sanctum" having our tea and biscuits, Mrs. Whistlebotham threw open the front windows of her daughter's house and played the early morning church program shamefully loud, turning up the volume for such stirring hymns as "Onward Christian Soldiers." Or just as we sat, basking in the golden glow of the smile before break-fast, there would be a knock at the back door. Mrs. Whis-tlebotham would be standing there with a cup in her hand, "Good morning, Mrs. Blount. I was wondering if you would be so kind as to loan us a cup of sugar? She wormed her way into the kitchen. "Oh, I'm terribly sorry I seem to have inter-rupted your breakfast." She didn't look sorry at all. "But food for the soul, Mr. Blount, is just as important as sausages!" Just as Father was about to put a succulent piece of sausage into his mouth, Mrs. Whistlebotham thrust a note card right under Father's nose bearing the times of all the Church of England Sunday services.

Mother hastily placed the cup of sugar into Mrs. Whis-tlebotham's hand and hustled her out the door, all the time Father muttering under his breath, "Put a drop of arsenic in it, Barbara, and let's have an end to it."

Or just when Father sat down to read the Sunday paper, the front doorbell rang and there she was cup in one hand and Bible in the other. Even the most holy of holies, after dinner nap time, was considered fair game. On this particular Sunday, it was my turn to be head masseur and hair comber. I had done my job well and Father was fast asleep and snoring contentedly. I could tell I was going to be trapped for a very long time, but I happened to look down and there by the side of the chair was Mother's bag of hair rollers. So, as a way of passing the time, I decided to give my father curly hair, and it wasn't long before his head was a helmet of large, pink, spiky rollers. I had just put the last roller in when the front doorbell rang. Father woke with a start. "Who's that?" he roared. John ran to the window. "It's Mrs. Weaselbum, Dad."

"Don't be rude!" Though it was my father who had coined the term "Weaselbum" on account of the fact that with her sharp, pointed nose and black, beady eyes set too close together, she looked remarkably like a weasel. Whenever he called her "Weeeeeaselbum," we were supposed to laugh uproariously, but whenever we said it, we were being rude.

"Right oh," said Father struggling to his feet, "I'm going to put an end to that woman's sanctimonious interference once and for all." He stumbled into the hallway, took hold of the doorknob, and pulled at it ferociously. Now, that door was a stubborn door and usually refused to open, but today it decided to cooperate and when Father pulled at it, it flew out of his hand and crashed into the hallway wall with a violent bang. "Arrrhhhh!" Father let out a roar of surprise and glowered down at Mrs. Whistlebotham from beneath the halo of large, pink, spiky hair rollers. The effect on Mrs. Whistlebotham couldn't have been more dramatic if Father had been wearing ladies' underwear!

"EEEEEEeeeeek!" She took an involuntary step backwards, dropped the china cup she was holding, and the bright red pages of that day's Bible texts fluttered around my father like flaming tongues of fire. Father must have thought she was ill or something of the sort, for he lunged towards her—ready to catch her should she faint. The sight of a middle aged man wearing hair rollers and lunging towards her was too much for Mrs. Whistlebotham's Christian sensibilities. She began to scream in earnest, turned on her heel, and scampered off down the garden path. Ignoring the gate completely, she leaped over the decorative hedge at the bottom of the garden, scampered across the street, and disappeared into the safety behind the white, lace curtains. A somewhat bemused but definitely delighted Father stumbled back into the living room. It wasn't until he scratched his head that he realized what all the commotion was about. I thought he might be angry, but not a bit of it. He started to laugh, a great roaring belly laugh that required several knee slappings before it subsided. Then, he dug into his pocket and gave me a half a crown for giving him the best laugh he'd had in weeks. I became a bit of a hero after that, for Mrs. Whistlebotham, convinced that Father's moral decline was complete and that he was beyond redemption, gave up her campaign and never darkened our doorstep again.

We were glad of it, no one more so than Father, and we settled back expecting the regular rhythm of our blissful Sundays to be restored. But it wasn't. Somewhere out there in the cosmos, the disturbance continued and—like the ripples on a pool of water—got larger and larger and things were never the same again.

Father lost his job. With four children to feed and clothe we were usually living hand-to-mouth. Without a job, it wasn't long before the situation became desperate. One Sunday we sat down to a dinner of rabbit. We didn't know it was rabbit and we certainly didn't realize it was our pet rabbit. If we had cleaned out the cage ourselves instead of leaving it to Mother, we would have found out sooner than we did. When we did discover the awful truth, John refused to put Billy Buttons, the hamster, in his cage but carried him around in his pocket.

"What have you got there?" Father demanded one day.

"Nothing," said John backing away, but Father rummaged in the bulging pocket.

"Eh up," said Father looking sadly at the twitching nose and whiskers, "it's not enough to fill a bloomin' sandwich." John heaved a sigh of relief and put the rejected lunchmeat back in his cage. Before my proud father was forced to turn to public assistance, he managed to find a job, but it was so far away he had to live away from home for two, sometimes three weeks at a time. Without his presence, we clanged around like empty vessels—out of step with ourselves and the world.

And all this happened in the year in which Mother became forty-three. On the day of her birthday, since Father was not home, we agreed to postpone the celebration until he was. However, we never did celebrate that birthday, for he had to come home early because he was ill. Mother, who always managed to find something to smile about, moved quietly about the house, her face pale and serious. Dr. Whitelaw was called and Father was taken immediately to hospital. Everybody panicked! "Eh up," Father often joked, "you have been at bloomin' death's door before the National Health Service'll take you into hospital."

It had only ever been a joke, but as it turned out, it happened to be true. Father went into the hospital on Thursday, and on the following Sunday he died. The heartbeat that had sustained the rhythm of our lives, the heartbeat that had created the sacred music to which we danced, was silenced. And just as that Romany gypsy so long ago had predicted, to all intents and purposes, my mother's life truly did come to an end.

It was some time before Mother felt able to return to her church. But eventually she did and when she came home that Wednesday night, it was with a gentle smile playing about her lips. As soon as she walked through the door, we wanted to ask, "Did you get a message? Did you get a message from

Father?" But we didn't for fear of bringing the tears to her eyes. In our silence, she read our thoughts. "The message I received was forget-me-nots." They had been Father's favorite flower. She had placed a small bunch of them on his coffin as it was lowered into the ground.

Early the following Sunday morning, there was a commotion down in the kitchen. Suddenly, from the bottom of the stairs we heard, "Eh up. Grub's up!" For the first time ever, Mother had cooked the Sunday breakfast, "the works:" eggs, bacon, sausage, tomatoes, and fried bread! We trundled down the stairs and gathered around the sacred altar. There was an empty place at the head and Mother sat at the tail. Just before we started to eat, Mother looked toward the empty place and smiled. And for a moment, time itself was suspended. There was no doubt in our minds that she could see Father smiling back at her. In the warmth of that smile, once more we knew we were blessed. Once more we felt the beat of my father's presence, and with it we knew we must create a new kind of rhythm and that one day we would dance to the echo of his song.

Home Delivery

I PICKED UP THE TELEPHONE and dialed long distance. My mother would have a heart attack—it was mid-week and usually I called her from the States on a Sunday morning. She would immediately panic and jump to the conclusion that something was wrong.

"Hello, Mum."

"What's wrong?"

"Nothing! I'm just calling to say I love you." There was a loud snort at the other end of the phone.

"The truth is I have this project to do for my master's program. I need to find out the story of my birth."

Personally, I thought the project was a waste of my time; since my mother was rhesus negative this meant that for safety's sake, just like my brother and sister, I had been born at Bond Street Hospital.

"I'm sure it's a boring story," I continued. "Contractions, pack the bag, and off to the hospital, where I expect Dad went to the waiting room and puffed on his Woodbine cigarettes until it was all over. End of story!"

"Well, that's how much you know," she said with a slightly superior attitude.

Then, for the next thirty minutes, I listened in amazement as my mother told me this story.

> I remember it was a bitterly cold night and your dad and I were huddled in front of the stove, which didn't seem to be throwing out any heat at all. Your dad was asleep in the easy chair, and I sat on the sofa doing some knitting—a little pair of bootees for you, I should think. Anyway, the labor pains started, but I ignored them for a while. There was no need to wake your dad too soon. I remember looking around—at the old sideboard and the worn, wooden table in the middle of the room. We didn't have much, just hand-me-downs we'd begged, borrowed, or stolen, but as your grandma used to say "Poverty is no excuse for slovenliness!" I'd made sure that everywhere was clean and tidy, so when Nurse Chadwick came, she would have nothing to complain about."

> It wasn't long before the pains increased in intensity and were settling into a regular rhythm. I looked at the time; it was ten o'clock. I hated to make your dad go outside on such a miserable night, but I had no choice.

> "Al!" He didn't move a muscle. He was so tired, poor

man. "Al!" I said it a little louder. He woke with a start and one eye sprang open.

It's time.

His other eye opened slowly, and without any sense of urgency, which was just like your dad, he pulled himself to his feet and went to the stove. He'd put two house bricks in the warming oven earlier, and he wrapped them in newspaper like two neat packages. "These will warm the bed for you, Barbara."

It didn't take him long. I heard him check on Richard and Katherine before he returned in his raincoat and cap. The raincoat was thin and insubstantial; it was nothing against the biting cold of the January night.

Have you got your scarf?

To set my mind at rest, he pulled open his coat—the scarf was like a brightly colored snake winding around his chest. He was a big man as you know—had a chest as big as a barrel—and the inadequacy of the woolen snake to keep out the chill just broke my heart.

He gave me a kiss and offered to put the water on to boil before he left, but I told him it was too soon, that I would have it ready by the time they got back.

Then, he disappeared into the cold night. He had an old bicycle—it was an antique affair that had belonged to his father—but it was sturdy and I'd filled the tires with air earlier in the day. I watched him out the window.

He gripped the handlebars tightly and lowered his head against the cold rain that had begun to fall, and then he disappeared up the street. Soon, the rain turned to ice, and I could imagine how it stung his cheeks—not that he was a stranger to bad weather. Working in the building trade, he had become hardened to it.

He told me later that the streets were deserted, and he saw no sign of man nor beast for the three miles he had to travel to Nurse Chadwick's house. When he got there, he took hold of the door knocker and gave it a hard rap, but there was no answer. He rapped even harder but there were still no signs of life. He admitted that he panicked a bit then and felt his heart thumping like a drum in his chest. He was about to throw rocks at the bedroom window when the door opened, and he said a woman appeared clutching her bath robe tightly at the neck. She didn't look like the midwife.

As you know, Nurse Chadwick was a sizeable, bonny woman with a riot of blond curly hair and plump cheeks. According to your dad, she was built like a small tank and had a bosom large enough to weep upon. This woman, he said, was pinched about the cheeks and looked as if she could do with a shoulder, possibly two to cry upon.

"Who is it?" the woman asked in a brisk, almost bossy voice, and your dad recognized the midwife instantly. He told her who it was and she became all business.

"Come in, Mr. Blount. I'll get dressed and get my bag," she said briskly. "Won't take me a minute!"

When she returned wearing her navy blue uniform with the starched white apron, your dad said her bosom seemed determined to present itself in a more capable light. However, it wasn't until Nurse Chadwick was wearing her district-nurse-hat that he began to feel better.

Then, they set off on their bicycles for the three mile ride home. Your dad used to make me laugh so much! He said when they reached the bottom of Sandpit Lane, that steep hill you kids loved to ride your trolley's down, poor Nurse Chadwick started to gasp and blow like an old steam engine. She told your dad he'd have to push her if she was to make it to the top, which was no easy task. Well, as he was struggling, who should come along but Patrick Hughes, the local bobby. He was a timid soul for all that he was a policeman. It probably frightened the poor man to death hearing all the puffing and blowing in the dark. But to give credit where it was due, as soon as he realized who it was, he abandoned his bicycle and pushed Nurse Chadwick the rest of the way up the hill—your dad said it was a primitive sort of police escort.

Without any other mishap, they arrived at the house. I could hear them in the kitchen whispering and bustling about. The next thing, they came upstairs—your dad leading the way with the boiling water. When Nurse Chadwick came in, I was shocked! She looked deathly ill.

"Don't worry, Mrs. Blount. Mr. Blount has agreed to help."

"Do what?" I was confused and couldn't imagine what use he might be in a delivery room.

"Nurse Chadwick says I must help with the instruments and such and make sure she doesn't faint." His face was so stricken, poor man, I had to laugh.

Then, Nurse Chadwick took control and seemed a little more like her old self. She sent your dad off to wash his hands and get the prep' box. She said the prep' box was very important especially with a rhesus negative mum and positive baby. Your dad groaned in response to this. When he came back he handed her the box and whispered, thinking I wouldn't hear, "Between you and me, I wasn't happy her having this one at home. Neither was her doctor, but she's that stubborn!"

With an imperious tone, she answered, "That's because she knows I'm a first class midwife. Why, you wouldn't doubt my capabilities would you, Mr. Blount?"

It was a rhetorical question—he wouldn't dare!

Then, she set to work. She timed the contractions and did a quick examination to see how far I'd progressed. The contractions were about five minutes apart, so it wouldn't be too long.

Your dad did everything Nurse Chadwick told him

and more: he mopped my brow with a wet face flannel, massaged my shoulders, and passed her the instruments she needed. I was amazed; he went and found more pillows and propped me up into a more comfortable position and seemed to know exactly where to rub my back to ease the pain. Then, when Nurse Chadwick told me I could push, he kept muttering words of encouragement and gave me his hand to squeeze. Just little things, but it was so comforting having him there.

Nurse Chadwick told me that the head was beginning to crown, and she told your dad to take a look. He looked scandalized, as if she has made an indecent proposal.

"Go on, man, it's your wife. It's your baby," said Nurse Chadwick and she couldn't help laughing at him, but as she stepped aside, she let out an anguished cry. Clutching her side, she collapsed onto the chair. Well, I panicked but not your dad.

"It's all right, Barbara. Everything is going to be all right," he kept saying, "I'm right here."

It was some time before Nurse Chadwick could answer. "Your husband's quite right. I'll just sit here and rest for a while. You and your husband will do the rest," she said, "Mr. Blount, you just get ready to catch that baby when it arrives!"

I wish you could have seen him, Jen. As if he'd been doing it all his life, he bent down and cupped those big, work-hardened hands of his like a cricketer ready to catch a low flying ball. I couldn't help but smile, but then the contractions came hard and fast and all I could do was push. Like an expert, your dad put his hand firmly on my belly as if guiding you toward the light. He told me to push gently. "That's right!" he kept repeating. "That's right, Barbara. I can see more of the baby's head. It's coming, Barbara. It's coming!" He was getting carried away by the moment, Jen, and sounded like an excited school boy waiting for his first ride on a train.

Then, with one last push, you finally arrived. You dropped like a little curled package into your dad's waiting hands. He'd never seen a baby like this before—covered in white paste and blood, and I wasn't sure how he would react. I needn't have worried, because he simply gazed down at you as if he couldn't quite believe what he was seeing. Then, he started breathing in great gulps of air and his whole body trembled. When he looked up, I could see his eyes had filled with tears and a sobbing sort of laugh escaped him. He always said that apart from me, he'd never seen anything quite as beautiful as a perfectly smooth, unblemished plastered wall. But I think now as he held you, he knew differently.

"She's beautiful," he whispered, and somewhere deep inside, my heart simply broke with love for this dear, good man.

My mother stopped for a moment, and I knew she was shedding some silent tears, but it wasn't long before she continued her story.

Suddenly, Jen, there was a great honking sound, which made us all jump—you included. Nurse Chadwick was blowing her nose and dabbing at her eyes, but she pulled herself together and said briskly, "Come along, Mr. Blount, there's more work to do." She showed your dad how to cut the umbilical cord and then he gave you your first bath. She tended to me and it wasn't long before your were nursing contentedly. Your dad went to make a cup of tea—I told him to put a drop of whiskey in his and Nurse Chadwick's—they both looked as if they needed it.

Katherine and Richard stumbled in looking bleary eyed, and you wouldn't have thought anything was wrong with Nurse Chadwick. She started bustling around quite like her old self. "Hello, my little chickens," she cried. "Come and see what your mummy's got."

They climbed onto the bed. Richard took one look at you and said your were ugly—well, he would, wouldn't he—and Katherine asked to hold you, but you let out such a blood curdling yell, she tossed you into the air and according to Richard, you bounced twice before I caught you. Now, I ask you, would any of this have happened at Bond Street Hospital? *No, I don't think so,* she said, answering her own question.

Of course, your dad went off to work as usual—couldn't afford to miss a day's work—and on the way he stopped off to tell Nellie Swan she'd be needed. Do you remember Nellie? A rough diamond of a woman, who worked for the welfare? She would do the cooking, the laundry, and housework until I was back on my feet.

So, Jen, in answer to your question, no, you were not born at Bond Street Hospital.

For a moment, I couldn't say anything—I couldn't find any words to make sense of what I was feeling, and so I said the first thing that popped into my head.

"What happened to Nurse Chadwick?"

"Oh, she was a real trooper. She jumped on her bicycle and pedaled the three miles back home. She'd no sooner arrived when she was rushed into the hospital for an emergency appendectomy. On her return home from the hospital, the first thing she did was to take a taxi at her own expense to our house to check up on us both. She said she'd neglected her duties for far too long. They just don't make them like that any more, our Jen."

As my mother talked, a rush of memories flooded through me. When my father died, it had taken me a long time to get over his death—I felt as if he had deserted me somehow. For months afterwards, I had the same dream: he was in the secret service on a mission which he could tell no one about. One day, wearing a navy blue military uniform, he came back and just like that everything was all right again. I suppose even as an adult, I had been living my life still needing to know that everything was going to be all right again. Finding out after so many years that my father had performed for me this, oh, so precious task seemed to come as a message directly from him.

Standing in my kitchen in Connecticut with the telephone in my hand, an umbilical cord of sorts connecting me to my mother, a strange sort of peace descended upon me. Once more I could feel the beat of my father's presence, once more I could feel his gentle touch, and once more I could feel his deep and abiding love.

As if lost in her own thoughts, my mother whispered softly, "So, thanks to your dad, Jen, everything was all right in the end, wasn't it?"

"Yes, Mum," I said with a smile. "In the end, everything is just fine."

Paying Homage

THE NURSING HOME had been built in the 60s and was in need of extensive renovation. However, when I walked in and sniffed the air, I could detect no whiff of urine under the scent of institutionalized food that hung in the air—a good sign, I thought.

A large woman, one of the staff, poked her head around the door of the office. She had black, spiked hair, multiple piercings, and sported a huge smile that revealed a broken front tooth and several gaps, the result, no doubt, of years of neglect and sporadic British dentistry. My brothers had looked into other more upscale nursing homes, but my mother wouldn't have been happy in such places. Hadrian House, by contrast, was in the village where she had lived most of her life, which meant that her neighbors and friends could visit easily. The caregivers here were local people, too, a

little rough around the edges, but—according to my brothers—
had compassionate hearts and unflagging good humor.

"I'm here to see my mother, Mrs. Blount. She moved in
recently." My mother wasn't expecting me. I had just arrived
from the States and had driven straight to Hadrian House
from Heathrow. My visit was a surprise—a distraction of sorts
to help smooth over the move from her bungalow into the
nursing home.

"You must be looking for Barbara. She's in the lounge."
She pointed the way. I thanked her and headed toward the
door.

As I walked in, a bow-legged old man with a walking
stick was leaving. "Hey up," he roared, "has my bloody car
been fixed yet?" For a moment, I thought he was addressing
me when suddenly the black, spiked hair reappeared, "Watch
your language, John. It won't be done until next week."

"Bugger!" he swore as he hobbled off. I found out later
that John had no car and wouldn't be going anywhere soon.

I glanced around the lounge, searching for my mother.
To the left, old ladies and old men resided in various states
of consciousness. Some stared vacantly ahead, others snored
loudly. One old lady was fast asleep. Her top dentures had
fallen out of her mouth and sat on her chin grinning like
a disembodied Cheshire cat. Another lady, her eyes, large
and forget-me-not blue, gazed vacuously in my direction. Her
beautiful face and indiscriminate smile warmed me—and
the room. To the right, it was a different story: the residents

chatted, read the paper, or tried—unsuccessfully—to watch the television. This was the "with it" section, and I was relieved to see my mother among their number.

My relief was somewhat short-lived. She sat hunched over in her wheelchair and her thin arms stuck out from the short sleeves of her purple blouse like chicken legs; her chin rested on her hollow chest and she snored quietly. She was a small, wizened shell of a woman who bore little resemblance to my mother. Sadly, I sat in the chair next to her and waited until she woke.

A lady opposite peered at me over the edge of her paper. She nodded toward my mother. "She saw the Queen Mother yesterday. Said she was wearing a yellow hat with feathers all around it—and the Queen Mother was waving to her. Standing behind her on top of the church wall, she said there was a full gospel choir singing 'Swing Low, Sweet Chariot'." She snorted, making it clear she resented my mother's presence in the "with it" section.

"Well," I responded haughtily, "If you're going to hallucinate a full gospel choir, why not invite the Queen Mother along to listen?" The woman didn't answer but quickly disappeared behind her paper.

And perhaps, I thought to myself, my mother wasn't hallucinating! A spiritualist all her life, she has always lived close to the world of the dead. Perhaps she actually did see the Queen Mother, a sort of royal Charon waiting to transport her from the world of the living to the world of the dead, with a gospel choir of angels ready to serenade her as she crossed.

Just then, Mother's eyes flickered open. "Hello, Mum," I said quietly.

It took a moment for her eyes to focus, but then she recognized who I was—another good sign.

"Oh, you're lucky, our Jen" she smiled as the tea and coffee trolley arrived. "You're just in time for elevenses." Taking my hand conspiratorially, she whispered, "They give us biscuits, too."

Her lack of surprise at my arrival was typical. Not long after I had moved to the States, I visited her without warning. Back then when she opened the front door, she just looked at me and tutted, "Well, I'd better put the kettle on." It was nice to know that, in this respect, Mum hadn't changed much.

Then, as everyone settled down to enjoy their tea or coffee, my mother made sure she had their undivided attention. "This is my daughter from Chicago," she announced with the intonation of someone whose daughter has recently received the Nobel Peace Prize. And it wasn't true. I no longer lived in Chicago, but Connecticut. She had known that for a long time, but she loved the idea of Chicago because it had a much more dangerous ring to it, as if I were some mobster's moll.

And she was not disappointed—an impressed chorus of "Well, I never!" rose up as one voice.

After tea, we visited her room, which did smell of urine. Oh, well.

"This is where I live now, our Jen," she said sadly.

The walls were bare; her move to the home had been somewhat rushed and my brothers, Richard and John, had time only to transport the necessities. Since my sister Katherine is in a wheel chair and couldn't help, I told my brothers I would take care of making her room more like home when I arrived. It was the least I could do after they had done so much. But in that bare room, my mother seemed frailer somehow—lost in a world and body that had betrayed her. No one looking at her now would see even the shadow of the impressive woman she had once been.

My mind wandered to the past. We had lived in a three-bedroomed council house on Charnwood Avenue in Thurmaston. My father worked in construction, a plasterer by trade. My mother didn't work outside the home. By all measures except one, we were poor. The house had an outside toilet next to the washhouse, which was a square, concrete room containing a sink, a *mangle*[9] and a dolly tub, a free standing zinc container shaped like a barrel where my mother did all the laundry.

One wash day, when I was probably about five years old, I went in to ask her an important question. Though she was lost a cloud of steam, I could see the impressive muscles of her arms bulging with the effort of thrusting the *podger* again and again into the tub filled with hot soapy water and bed sheets.

---

9 Wringer

The podger was a long stick with a copper bowl on the end with holes around its rim and shaped liked a toilet plunger. Really it was just a step up from rubbing the laundry between two boulders by the side of a river.

"What is it, my little chicken?" She had abandoned the podger and with one hand was now using a pair of wooden tongues to haul the waterlogged sheets out of the tub and feed them between the rollers of the mangle. With the other hand, she turned the handle of the great wheel with its vicious inter-locking green teeth, which made the rollers go round. We were terrified of the mangle because years ago, those vicious green teeth had bitten off my grandfather's thumb.

"Muuumm? Can I keep what's in my pocket?"

She paused and straightened. "Well, I suppose that all depends on what it is. Can I see it?"

I hesitated and then produced the field mouse. "His name's Malcolm."

My mother looked at the small creature and then at my earnest face. "Do you know where Malcolm's mummy is?" I shook my head. "Don't you think his mummy will miss him if he came to live with us?" I hadn't thought of this. "Why don't you play with him the rest of the day? Then, you can let him go back to his mummy in time for tea."

I nodded my head in agreement. "You'll love it, Malcolm," I said enthusiastically. "My mum makes the best toys in the world!" And she did. I took him into the kitchen where we played with the large can of sand that came with an old battered tray and a bizarre assortment of bowls and spoons. As I poured and mixed and spilled, Malcolm ran up and down the miniature Sahara Desert I created. When he lost interest, I took him for a walk on the tin can stilts my mother had made by turning the cans upside down and attaching a long wire handle to each. "We'll break our bloomin' necks, Malcolm," I laughed imitating my mother.

Before I let him go, I took him for a ride on Dobbin. We had two ponies, Dobbin and Hercules, which Mother had made from two discarded sawhorses. She had made two saddles fashioned from old towels, stirrups and reins made from neighbors' discarded dog leashes, and had attached wooden hobby-horse heads replete with woolen manes—at the other end were long woolen tails.

Mum made everything magical. Years later when I visited with my own children, Ben and Andrew, they, too, fell under her spell.

"Hi, Grandma!" yelled Ben when we first arrived. "We just came on a bus filled with escaped convicts!"

"Well, we'll have to call you Pip from *Great Expectations* then!" she exclaimed, which pleased the boys to no end.

"They were *released* convicts," I explained quickly, but no one was listening to me.

"Dave's coming to Chicago to baby-sit for us, isn't he Andrew?"

"Oh, I'm sure your daddy will love that!" laughed my mother.

Andrew pulled on her skirt. "Can we go outside to play, Grandma?"

"Of course you can, my little chickens!" They'd never been called that before and they ran off giggling. "Just remember," she yelled, "you mustn't play on people's lawns. You must play in the street."

Their heads spun around and their eyes sparkled. In one swift stroke, all my years of careful parenting unraveled before my eyes. Later that night, before they climbed into bed, she took them into the back garden. She put her hands to her lips. "Shhsss! Just watch!" She held a saucer of milk. "Horace! Come on, my baby!" Soon, they heard a snuffling sound and out of the darkness a small hedgehog, a creature my boys had never seen before, shuffled across to my mother's outstretched hand, nudged it gently, and then started to lap up the milk. The boys' eyes were as wide as the saucer!

I smiled as I thought of this and once more felt the magic of my own childhood return. I looked down at my mother. How had this frail woman managed to conjure it all and do all the cooking and cleaning for a family of six—seven when granddad came to live us? Not to mention ironing all that laundry using an old metal iron she heated on the top of the stove. She ironed everything—even our underwear.

As if she had followed my mind into the past, my mother said, "I was just thinking about poor old Richard. Do you remember when he got the cane?" The disciplinarian's cane was a thin whippet of a stick made of rattan that sliced through the air with a threatening hiss. I remembered it with a shudder.

⊁

At four-fifteen on that afternoon, Katherine and I burst into the kitchen, which was filled with the aroma of home-made Chelsea buns. "Wash your hands and sit down," cried Mother. "The buns will be ready soon." We did as we were told and soon a mound of buns—the icing melting down their warm sides—appeared on a plate.

"Where's Richard," my mother wanted to know. Just then, he arrived, pale-faced and serious. "What on earth's the matter?" But he said nothing and went up to his room. That night, he ate little supper, and when we were all in bed, we heard him sniffling in the dark. The next morning he tried to eat some toast, but threw up instead. Mum put her arms around him. "What's wrong my little chicken? Surely you can tell your mummy," she crooned. Richard broke down, "Mr. Atkinson," he sobbed, "is giving me the cane today."

She didn't ask what Richard had done to deserve it; instead, she threw on her hat and coat, put John in his pushchair, and accompanied us to school, which had never happened before. Even on our first day of infant school, she had kissed us goodbye at the garden gate and sent us on our way with all the other kids from the street. But not today! After she deposited us in the play ground, she marched inside to Mr. Atkinson's room where, as she told Father later, she gave him a piece of her mind. "I don't want to know what Richard did yesterday to get the cane, because I'm sure he deserves it, but to make him, or any child, worry for a whole day and night. Well, that is just downright cruel! It's unworthy of you."

To his credit, Mr. Atkinson looked shamefaced and withdrew the threat to cane Richard.

"Yes, you will cane him, Mr. Atkinson! If a child of mine has done something wrong, then he should be punished. Just cane him right away next time."

My mother sighed at the memory and then she brightened, "It's nearly lunch time! And guess what? Spotted dick for pudding today!" This British delicacy is a steamed sponge pudding made from flour, milk, sugar, beef suet, and raisins—hence the "spotted"—where the "dick" came from I've no idea, but it was our favorite pudding when we were children. How could I resist?

When we entered the dining room, my mother told me to push her toward a table at the back of the room where all the "with-its" were seated. It was full. She glared at the interloper. "You're sitting in my seat! I always sit here." Her voice rose a little.

"We've been telling her, Barbara, but she won't move," the others at the table assured my mother. The small wiry woman ignored them and held her ground. I could see immediately that this was more than a battle over a seat—this was a battle against the creeping effects of dementia, a claim to mental acuity to which this woman and my mother only tentatively clung. Barely able to walk, Mother struggled to her feet. Immediately, I knew things were going to get ugly. Though she was kind and generous to a fault, you just didn't mess with my mother.

After we were grown up and had left home, every Saturday morning Mother caught the bus into town to do her weekly grocery shopping at the Leicester City Market—and, if the truth be known, to stop and enjoy half a pint of bitter with a friend at the pub before she came home.

One Saturday morning as the bus was heading into town, it made a stop along Melton Road, and two unsavory looking teenagers boarded the bus. Their greasy hair fell in long stringy tendrils down the backs of their battered leather jackets. As soon as they sat down, the pair lifted their legs over the seatbacks in front of them so that their feet rested on the vacant seats. They leaned back like kings, and their eyes, narrow slits in their ferret-thin faces, flickered around the bus just daring someone to challenge them. No one did. Gradually, the bus became crowded and the only remaining seats were those occupied by the teenagers' feet. At the next bus stop, an old lady climbed on board. She looked at the teenagers, at the potentially empty seat, but was either too timid or too frightened to ask them to move their feet. My mother was neither. "So, did you buy four tickets, then?" she demanded pointedly.

Sneering, they turned to her. "What do you mean, luv?" The word "luv" was a threat.

"I mean," she said, leaning forward so that they were sure to hear, "you're taking up four seats while this lady has to stand!"

Suddenly, a man from the back of the bus yelled, "That's right, me duck, you tell 'em!" Immediately, Mother shot down this potential ally, "And you can shut up! You didn't say anything, did you?" Turning once more to the young men, she hissed in an icy voice no thicker than a scalpel, "Now, you take your feet down, or I'll take them down for you."

A loud cheer erupted from the crowded bus. Faced with a united front, the offenders, directing a hostile look in my mother's direction, reluctantly removed their feet. The old lady sat down and, inspired by my mother's example, pumped her fist triumphantly into the air. This prompted another roar of approval. When everyone got off the bus in town, two burly men walked behind my mother and the old lady so that the teenagers wouldn't bother them again.

My mother, as if channeling the energy of this memory, trembled as she prepared to launch her verbal assault upon the wiry interloper. Fortunately, the woman with the black, spiked hair appeared and gently guided Mother back into her wheelchair. "Barbara, I thought just for today we'd set up a special table for you and your daughter," she lied, "so you can have a little bit of privacy."

Special treatment! My mother brightened visibly, but she turned once more to the impostor. "Just for now!" she shouted in a voice still containing a hint of the scalpel. "Don't you forget, that's my seat, and I'll want it back tonight!"

Spike—that's what they called her, and I exchanged conspiratorial looks. She smiled her broken-tooth smile, and I beamed my gratitude.

After our secluded lunch, John, the bow-legged man with the walking stick, accompanied us out of the dining room and was once more on a quest to find his fictitious car, which he discovered still wasn't ready. "I'm going for a bloody smoke, then," he swore. "Do you want a fag, Barbara?"

My mother looked affronted and, if she had been standing, would have drawn herself up to her full height. "I do not smoke," she claimed imperiously. I burst out laughing. My mother has smoked more that a pack a day since she started smoking at the age of fourteen. Oh, she had tried many times to give up and one time had taken to sucking on Nuttall's Mintoes[10] instead. She knew she was a lost cause when one day, after she had popped a mint in her mouth, she found herself with a match in her hand trying to light it.

When she developed asthma in her late forties, the doctors insisted she give up, and to her credit, she pretended that she had. Although we never actually caught her smoking, years later when her gas fire had to be removed, the workmen

---

10   Once a world-famous sweet made in Doncaster.

discovered a mountain of ash and cigarette butts in the exhaust space at the back. They said it was a miracle the whole house hadn't gone up in flames. When she stayed with us in Chicago for two months and we turned on the air conditioning for the first time, a plume of ash shot out of the vent in the bathroom covering Ben, my twelve-year-old son, who appeared at the top of the stairs the very reincarnation of Marley's ghost.

My mother's caustic comment brought me back to the present. "I don't know why you're laughing, our Jen. I gave up smoking years ago."

"Right," I agreed. *Why stop pretending now,* I thought?

We spent a quiet afternoon, and just before supper I took her into the dining room a little early so she'd be sure to get her seat, and then I drove the short distance to her bungalow. There was a For Sale in the front garden—I never realized until then just how sad some for sale signs can be; this one signaled the end of an era.

The next day I packed up the car with small pieces of furniture, a couple of lamps, a few knickknacks, and her photographs. The walls of her little bungalow were covered with them; the last photograph I took down was a picture of my father holding me as a baby. Katherine and Richard sat at his feet and Mother stood beaming at his side. John was still just a twinkle in my dad's eye. My father had died over forty years ago, but every Saturday when Mother went into town, she bought a bunch of flowers and put them into a vase on the dresser underneath this photograph—she made a sort of shrine of it. He was the love of her life. So, I picked a bunch of flowers from her garden before my final trip to Hadrian House.

The janitor helped me haul everything up to her room. While I arranged the furniture and cleaned out the commode with lemon-smelling disinfectant, he hung all the pictures. The photograph of my father went above the small dresser at the end of her bed. I arranged the flowers in a vase and placed them beneath the picture—they would be the first things she would see when she woke up. Last of all, I placed a small potpourri on the window ledge—it smelled of forget-me-nots, my father's favorite flower. Then, I went to fetch my mother.

"Tadaaa," I said with a flourish when we entered her room.

"Jennie, it looks lovely!" She made me push her over to the dresser where she gazed at the photograph.

"He was lovely, was your dad, our Jen," she sighed sadly.

"I know, Mum."

"You know after Dad died, Val was always trying to set me up with someone—you remember Val, right? Taught me everything I needed to know when I started work at Winterton's hosiery factory. I had no experience and Mr. Winterton was taking a chance on me. If it hadn't have been for Val, I would have lost the job. She saved my life and she made me laugh. Every day, Val waited for me to get off the bus and we'd walk to work together. Well, we got to work one day, and there was a big hole in the *pavement*[11] just outside the factory—it was wide and deep and probably should have had some yellow tape around it. Val took one look and said, 'Eh up, Barbara, I think you've got yourself a man trap!' Well, we both laughed and thought no more about it, but at the end of the day when we left work, there was a man from the water-works bent over and fixing a pipe. 'Eh up, Barbara,' laughed Val, 'you've bloomin' well caught one!' Looking at the man's huge bum sticking up in the air, I added, 'And he's a big 'un, too!' Val and I roared with laughter. The poor man had no idea what was going on."

Then, my mother turned from the dresser. "Course I only ever joked about finding someone else—I was never serious. I loved your dad too much."

"I know, Mum."

"It was a blind date," she reminisced, and love almost at first sight—did you know that our Jen?"

"No," I lied. "Tell me what happened." And then my mother, who could barely remember what had happened yesterday, told her story with astounding clarity.

She settled down in her chair.

Well, Peggy Shepherd, George Palmer, and Albert [that was my dad] knocked on the door at Aunty Lily and Uncle Harry's, which was where I was living at the time. I opened the door and took one look at Albert and decided I didn't like him. In his deep blue overcoat with its tie belt and padded shoulders, he looked like a

11. Sidewalk

wide-boy, as we used to say—too sharp for his own good and definitely not my type. But before this thought had time to fully register, Sabu—you remember Uncle Harry had a pet monkey, right? Well, Sabu shot through the air, over my head, and landed on Al's shoulder.

I suppose I should have warned them about the monkey. Peggy squealed, George Palmer squeaked, but not your dad. He started to laugh, which delighted Sabu so much he jumped up and down wildly on Dad's shoulder all the time pulling Dad's hair, which was unfashionably long—another point against him. Sabu didn't agree with my opinion. He wrapped his tail around Dad's head and started to groom him. I had never seen him do that with anyone else but your Uncle Harry! It was then I noticed your dad's eyes were the same deep blue as his overcoat. And that's when I fell in love with him. Just like that. We went for a walk along the river, and we didn't even hold hands, Jen. That's how it was back then. We went for lots of walks along the river.

She smiled at the memory and then continued her tale.

Our first date alone, we went to the pictures, but I had left it a bit late getting ready. At the time, Aunty Lily lived on Filbert Street, the home of the Leicester City Football Club. The game had just finished and the busses were so crowded, I couldn't get on. I was over an hour late and when I got to the cinema, there was no sign of your dad. I was wondering what to do when a bus pulled up and Al jumped off—he'd had to work late. He was surprised that I had waited so long. He said,

"Now I know you must really love me." I didn't tell him the truth until we were engaged, and he said I'd got him under false pretenses!

Well, we had to wait a while for the next show to begin and before we took our seats, your dad took off his overcoat. It was the first time I'd seen him without it—and I discovered that I had been wrong about the padded shoulders. I fell in love with him all over again. It was a good job because just as the film started, a couple took a seat in front of us. The man, who sported an ill-fitting toupee, was much older than the woman; she was wearing a fur coat and clutched a large box of chocolates. "They're not married," whispered Albert. "He's her fancy man."

I was sure they would hear your dad, but before I could tell him to be quiet, the man sat down, and the arm of his seat broke off. He fell out into the aisle, rolled down the sloping floor, and disappeared into the darkness. Dad let out a roar of laughter and couldn't stop—even when the poor man groped his way back to his seat and glared angrily at him. Eventually, Dad was laughing so hard, the couple had to move.

We'll be thrown out! I hissed, but he still couldn't stop laughing. Even on the bus home, he kept roaring with laughter until at length the whole bus—even though they didn't know what he was laughing at—joined in. And I never stopped laughing, our Jen, all the years we were married.

"Not, that is," she added sadly, "until he died."

She paused.

"I still miss him every day."

I looked down at her—she was smiling sadly and gazing into the distance at pictures only she was privileged to see. Once again I looked at her thin arms, which stuck out from the short sleeves of her blouse like chicken legs, but in them I was now able to see the ghost of the robust arms that had once been the arms of the lover, the mother, and the friend. And I knew that it wouldn't be long before she would slip forever into the pictures and stories of her past. I put my arm around her and held her close. Oh, not to keep her in this world, for that would have been cruel, but because I knew what a great honor it had been to have had her in my life.

Strangely, as I held her, I began to think of the bow-legged old man, the lady with the Cheshire-cat-teeth, the wiry interloper, the woman with the forget-me-not blue eyes, and even the surly woman behind the newspaper. I now understood that they, too, had lived lives every bit as vibrant as my mother's. Their physical and mental weaknesses, like my mother's, were a testament to the gauntlet they had long ago thrown to the world. If we are lucky, we are able to pick up the gauntlet, and the only way we can do that is by listening to their stories and sharing their memories. In the end, it is the only way we can pay homage to their courage, their endurance, and their humanity.

Earnest

EARNEST: SERIOUS, ZEALOUS, NOT TRIFLING, ARDENT.
According to this dictionary definition, I was a very earnest
young woman. Being earnest, everything I did, I took very
seriously, especially being pregnant. Obsessed with doing
everything right, I was determined to produce the perfect
baby, I was determined to raise the perfect child, and I was
determined to return to my ... OK, maybe not so perfect,
but not so bad, pre-pregnant shape. I read every book the
library possessed on pregnancy and child rearing practices,
and it wasn't long before I became somewhat of an expert.
In the checkout lines in supermarkets, I would look with a
certain disdain at toddlers throwing temper tantrums. Having
studied, I knew that with just the right kind of handling, such
scenes could easily be avoided.

But right now, my focus was on being pregnant. Two

things kept cropping up that caused me concern: stretch marks and varicose veins. I made up my mind not to have either. In an effort to avoid stretch marks, I lathered copious amounts of cocoa butter into my stomach every morning and evening in the naive belief that my stomach would return to its perfectly flat, smooth, pre-pregnant condition. The fact that my efforts were doomed to failure did not for one moment occur to me. Perhaps, I should point out that my husband is six foot three, and I a mere five foot three. Eventually, the baby had nowhere to grow but out—further out, as it transpired, than my skin was capable of stretching.

I was somewhat more successful with varicose veins. Varicose veins, I found out, are caused by blood getting trapped behind the valves that help propel the blood through the veins. The trapped blood forms into large clotted lumps which bulge out distorting the vein so that the leg looks as if it has twisted coils of blue rope buried just beneath the skin. My mission was obvious. I had to stop the blood from getting trapped. This, I read, could be done by bathing the legs in cool water both night and morning, massaging them regularly, and elevating the feet above the head at frequent intervals during the day.

I was a very earnest young woman. I kept to this regimen every day for the duration of my pregnancy. At the time, I taught in a junior high school where elevating my feet above my head proved to be difficult but not impossible. During my planning period and lunch break, I disappeared into the small staff bathroom. It was so small that I could sit comfortably on the toilet seat and rest my feet in an elevated position against the opposite wall. As I gradually grew bigger, however, this position slowly became snugger. Eventually, it became so snug that one day I was wedged in tight and couldn't free my legs without the danger of falling sideways onto the floor. I was stuck!

A group of noisy students walked past the door. I banged loudly on the wall and shouted for help. One brave soul approached.

"Is there anyone in there?"

I decided to ignore the inanity of the question.

"Bob?" I knew it was Bob Westlake. With only two hundred and twenty-five students in the entire school, it wasn't difficult to pick out Bob's voice.

"It's Mrs. Munro. I need your help."

"Oh, God!"

I knew what he was thinking. "It's all right. I'm not in labor. Just go and get Luther." Luther was the janitor.

"Oh, well, in that case, I'll need a pass."

"Perhaps you would like me to write it on toilet paper and slip it under the door?" I was uncomfortable and beginning to lose my patience.

"Do you need a pen?"

"Just go and get Luther!" I exploded.

Luther arrived. "Mrs. Munro?"

"Yes"

"Are you all right?"

"I'm stuck!"

There was a long pause while Luther considered the various positions in which I might be stuck.

"You will have to remove the lock," I explained patiently, "and help me out."

There was another long silence while Luther searched for the appropriate words.

"Will I need a blanket?"

There was now a long silence while I considered the various uses to which a blanket might be put. Sensing my dilemma, Luther asked, "Er—Mrs. Munro, are you decent?"

I quickly put Luther's mind to rest, and he set to work. Luther unscrewed the lock and the door swung inward. I was now trapped behind the door. The only way for Luther to get me out was to take the door off its hinges, which he did in no time. Then, like a valiant knight rescuing a rather rotund princess, Luther picked me up and carried me to freedom.

Now, this was in the days when individual classroom walls were considered anti-educational. It was as close to a one-room schoolhouse as you could get in the modern era. As soon as we stepped into the main teaching area, two hundred and twenty-five students leaped to their feet and gave us a standing ovation. The principal, not to be out done, insisted that I go home and rest for the remainder of the afternoon.

As the pregnancy advanced, my husband, Eric, and I had certain decisions to make about the birth itself. We certainly wanted to take Lamaze classes and "enjoy" all the advantages of a natural birth. Then we were asked if we would like a Leboyer birth where immediately upon arrival the baby is placed upon the mother's stretch-mark free stomach while Dad cuts the umbilical cord before plunging the baby into warm water to give him his first bath.

"Lamaze begins with an "L," and so does Leboyer," Eric pointed out to no one in particular. "We may as well do it." The workings of the engineer mind never fail to amaze me! And then, of course, there was La Leche League. Three "L's"— how could I resist?

At the first meeting, while mothers discussed nursing bras and the wisdom of wearing patterned blouses when breast feeding, I watched a two-year-old clamber onto his mother's lap, turn his baseball cap around so that the peak was at the back before hoisting his mother's sweater and tucking in. Across the room, a large, impressive woman was effortlessly nursing three-year-old twins. There was no false modesty here. Bare breasts were the order of the day. I could recognize zealots when I saw them, and I felt immediately at home.

I read the La Leche League manual from cover to cover, concentrating for the moment on "nipple" preparation. Apparently, my first task was to toughen them up so that they could withstand the vigorous sucking of a newborn and beyond. First, I had to twiddle them regularly, which I did. I felt as if I were tuning myself into some sort of cosmic maternal radio station. However, the very best thing according to the manual was to expose the nipples daily to the benefits of the fresh, open air. I paused, allowing the image of myself bare-breasted and pregnant to skip across my suburban back lawn. I squelched it immediately, not wishing to offend the Lutheran family who lived across the way.

But I was a very earnest young woman and if fresh air was what my nipples needed, then fresh air was what they would get. It didn't take long for me to discern a workable solution. I discovered that if I knelt by my bedroom window, I would be just the right height for my breasts to rest on the window ledge. I could push the window up just enough to allow the fresh air to bathe my exposed nipples.

There was only one problem to this solution. The bedroom window of our next door neighbor's house directly faced ours. Unlike the Lutherans across the way, these neighbors didn't seem to be of a religious nature, but I still didn't want to shock or cause offense. The husband, however, did work nights, and as a result, I had never seen the bedroom blinds in any other position than closed. In the interest of tough nipples, I decided the risk was worth it.

One day as I was enjoying the toughening effects of a particularly boisterous breeze, the bedroom blinds next door shot up. Instead of ducking out of the way, which would have been the sensible thing to do, I froze. The husband looked across the narrow divide that separated our two houses and his eyes, not surprisingly, went immediately to my bare breasts. He slowly lifted his head and our eyes met. I waited for a look of shock, or horror, or at least surprise to contort his features. To my relief, none was forthcoming. Instead, he looked totally bewildered as if trying to figure out exactly what he was seeing. I seized the moment and waved in what I hoped was a rather jolly manner. A jolly wave, I determined, was not the sort of wave a bare-breasted young woman might give. It worked! He waved back distractedly, as if still trying to work out what it was I might or might not be wearing. Then, I experienced a moment of sheer inspiration. I reached for a tissue from my bedside table and began conscientiously to dust the window frame. Eventually, still looking hopelessly bewildered, he gave a shrug of defeat and slowly lowered the blinds.

In the interest of maintaining friendly relations with my neighbors, I decided my nipples were tough enough for the ordeal ahead, and I kept them away from the window ledge for the few remaining weeks of my pregnancy.

In due time, contractions began. The suitcase had long since been packed and we set off for the hospital. I feel I should mention the contents of the suitcase at this point. I had read in a magazine that one should avoid taking a maternity outfit to the hospital for the trip home with the new baby. After all, they reasoned, everyone by this time is thoroughly sick and tired of maternity clothes. No, they said take a nice, non-maternity but comfortable outfit. "It will lift your spirits," they assured the hapless reader. I packed a pant outfit which had an elasticized waist and zipper and would, I felt sure, be roomy enough to accommodate my non-pregnant girth.

When it came time to get dressed to go home after delivering the baby, I looked down at the large wad of red-streaked flesh that had once been my perfectly, flat, smooth stomach. I was able to pull it out, fold it over, and then force-feed it into the hopelessly narrow opening of the pants. Needless to say, there was nothing remotely uplifting about this experience. My spirits—along with the folded-flap of flesh—were securely and painfully wedged behind the straining teeth of the zipper.

But I digress. Contractions began, and we set off for the hospital. When we arrived, we signed in and a nurse escorted us to our room. We had no sooner settled in when my water broke. I think I do not exaggerate when I say cascades of water shot into the room and wouldn't stop. "Bring buckets!" the excited nurse shrieked. I half expected the baby to come shooting out right then and there singing, "I'm riding along on the crest of a wave and the sun is in the sky!"[12] But no such luck! Two buckets and many towels later, contractions began in earnest and it wasn't long before I decided to forego the "natural" part of this birth. My husband, the coach, encouraged me by modeling various breathing techniques and suggested I try some of them. I told him in no uncertain terms exactly where he could stuff his breathing techniques, grabbed hold of his hospital gown, and hissed, "Get ... the ... nurse!"

12.   From *Riding on the Crest of the Wave* by Ralph Reader. Reproduced with permission.

A perky young thing arrived and looked at me indulgently. "Oh, I'm sure *we've* got a long way to go yet, Mrs. Munro—but let's have a peek and see how *we're* doing." The nurse's head disappeared and then quickly popped up between my knees. "Oh, the baby's head has crowned. That was quick! *Too quick* was the inference and I felt immediately guilty. "Dr. Ryan isn't here yet." Then, she allowed herself a small smile. "Don't push!" Not pushing is akin to holding back twenty wild horses all intent on galloping in the same direction. But being the earnest young woman I was, I gamely took hold of the reins while the nurses and my husband galloped with me into the delivery room.

After what seemed like an eternity, the doctor arrived and gave me permission to push. *Yee hah!* I let go of the reins. I pushed, I strained, I groaned.

At length, the doctor peered at me over his hospital mask. "Three more good pushes, Jen, and you're done."

I felt as if I would somehow fail the course if I took more than the prescribed three pushes, so I put everything I had into them. Muscles strained, blood vessels in my eye balls exploded, and the baby shot out so fast, the doctor had to catch him like a football. I could see it took considerable restraint for him not to dash the baby to the ground and shout, "Touchdown!"

The baby was then placed on my stomach. He was not crying, but was making these odd little panting sounds. "Is he all right?" I demanded. I looked up to find that the doctor, too, was making the same odd little panting sounds.

"Don't worry," he explained breathlessly, "It always happens when they arrive so quickly," but whether he meant himself or the baby was not entirely clear.

When Eric had finished cutting the umbilical cord, he then gave the baby his Leboyer bath. "He's doing the backstroke, Jen," he announced proudly.

Then, I nursed the baby on my suitably tough nipples and stared earnestly at my son. He was red, wrinkled, and perfect. I had done it. I had produced the perfect baby. I gazed down at him, filled with an overwhelming love that poured down my cheeks in a river of tears. So what if my stomach had the consistency of gelatin and texture of orange peel, at least I was able to comfort myself with the certain knowledge that after all the reading I had done, raising Ben would be a piece of cake!

Read My Lips

I HAD JUST GIVEN BIRTH TO OUR FIRST CHILD, a boy. My husband, Eric, leaned toward me and took hold of my face gently. An engineer by trade, he was not given to emotive endearments, but I knew this time must be different. Pulling his face mask down, he peered at me intently, and whispered tenderly, "Read my lips, Jen. No pets!"

Now, before we were married, we had not even discussed whether or not we wanted children, let alone whether those phantom children would be allowed to have pets. In my chaotic household growing up, we had always had pets: there was Sammy, the gold fish, which we had for years, until he died mysteriously while we were away on vacation. Mrs. Hyman, our neighbor, had taken care of him while we were gone and on his death had replaced him with a look-alike substitute, but my mother knew immediately that this was an impostor. Whenever, she had spoken to the original model, our Sammy had hovered at the front of the bowl, listening intently to every word she said.

Then, there was the blue rubber ball—a substitute for a dog, which at the time, we could ill afford. My dad had drilled a hole right through the middle of the ball, and inserted a string so that we could take "Spot" for walks. Our greatest delight was to bounce it, yank on the leash, and shout "Come!" Immediately, Spot would leap into our open arms, a model of canine obedience.

By comparison, Sooty, our real dog, who arrived years later, was a disappointing substitute that doggedly refused to heed even the simplest of commands. Should anyone leave the door open, he shot out of the house and disappeared for days at a time—only to return smelling of dog turds and sporting an obscene grin.

Tommy the tortoise was my favorite—if we waited long enough, he would actually come when we called him. We did have a rabbit for a while, but since dire straits forced us to eat it, I don't think it really counts.

Anyway, the point is that children and pets, at least in my mind, were inextricably linked. Negotiating this fundamental philosophical difference between my husband and me, would require great diplomacy on my part.

To this end, we started off with a brightly colored ceramic parrot in a macramé cage that I hung in the kitchen. By this time, we had two boys, five and two, who fed it peanuts while

I kept up a constant chorus of "Pretty Polly," "Finish your breakfast," "Don't hit your brother," and a whole host of other useful parental directives which—because they came from the parrot—were religiously obeyed. Of course, the willing suspension of disbelief and the boys' fleeting obedience gradually disappeared at the same rate the uneaten peanuts accumulated in the bottom of the cage. It was obvious that a real pet was required.

A goldfish seemed a simple way to begin—and Eric, though not thrilled, agreed, failing to recognize this as the thin end of a mighty wedge. Nancy Bell, so named after Ben's first love in kindergarten, was installed in the penthouse of fish bowls, which was replete with plastic seaweed and a Davy Jones's locker. At the request of the boys, it was ensconced on the top of the dresser in their bedroom—a mistake I now realize.

In order to gaze at Nancy Bell together—a feat that could not be achieved by using the chair I had provided for their individual viewing pleasure—Andrew pulled out the dresser drawers into a series of steps, which they both proceeded to climb. The force of the dresser falling on top of the boys catapulted Nancy Bell and her glass bowl into the air. Hitting the wall with a massive crash, the glass shattered and Nancy Bell fell to the floor where she floundered, gasping for breath in a fast disappearing puddle of water.

Alerted by the bloodcurdling screams, I dashed upstairs and, I think this establishes beyond any reasonable doubt the suspect quality of my parenting capabilities, took one look at Nancy Bell as she flopped around in a desperate attempt to come to terms with this capricious turn of events, and promptly saved her rather than my children. Only when she was swimming happily in a saucepan of water in the kitchen, did I return to rescue the boys. They gave a somewhat feeble cheer when I told them Nancy Bell lived.

Though they loved Nancy Bell, they pointed out to their father the limitations of having a goldfish as a pet and—by contrast—the enormous benefits of furry ones. And so when they asked for a hamster and gerbil respectively, Eric, relieved that they hadn't asked for a dog, caved in. The hamster and gerbil did indeed fill that deep-seated need all children have to nurture a small, defenseless creature—until one day when they were in the utility room cleaning the animals' cages. Andrew's gerbil escaped and disappeared behind the washer and dryer, and I was summoned to help retrieve it. "Right, you stand by the washer, Ben. Andrew, you stand by the dryer. When I bang on the washer, both of you get ready to catch it when it shoots out! Right?"

"We'll need our baseball mitts," they decided and ran to get them. On their return, they crouched into position like seasoned players.

"One, two, three!" I pounded on the side of the washer probably a little too enthusiastically and a black missile shot out from under the machine. Ben let out a startled cry of alarm and leaped into the air. Defying the law of gravity, he hung suspended for a moment. Only when Blackie was directly beneath him, did Ben begin his inevitable, deadly descent. We closed our eyes and waited until we heard the anticipated crunch.

Andrew let out a wail of despair, ran into the garage, and locked himself in his dad's car. Ben, sobbing, ran upstairs and locked himself in his bedroom. Meanwhile, the gerbil, caught in the throes of death, lay on its back with its legs flailing, blood pouring from its mouth. Now, whether from the horror of the situation or from feeling totally inadequate to the task, I was suddenly gripped by an uncontrollable fit of laughter, and I collapsed in a heap upon the dryer—another testament to my pathetic parenting skills. By the time I recovered, the gerbil lay dead upon the floor. Rallying at last, I found a suitable box and managed to coax both boys from their respective hiding places.

The ritual of a funeral seemed to calm everyone. Ben and Andrew retrieved green plastic grass from the Easter decorations and used it to line the "coffin." Together, they dug a hole under the apple tree and placed the box inside. They replaced the dirt and sod, erected a Popsicle stick cross on the grave, and Andrew gave a short eulogy: "I still love you, Gunga Din, and want you to know that Ben didn't do it on purpose. Amen." The boys gave one another one of their rare hugs. Harmony was restored.

Without Gunga Din as a companion, Hercules, the hamster, expired a short time later and once more the boys were back on the "we need a pet" trail. To Eric's dismay, the local children's farm where Ben and Andrew belonged to the 4-H Club was looking for a good home for a little Dutch rabbit. "And it comes with a cage and everything," said Andrew, as if this sealed the deal.

Eric groaned and the rabbit moved in. We called her Minnehaha. A little under two weeks later she gave birth to six babies. "We should have called her Minnewhorewhore," Eric muttered under his breath when he heard the news.

We now had seven rabbits and to make matters worse, when we attended the local 4-H fair the following week, Andrew asked if he could buy raffle tickets. I said, "Sure!" The prizes were stereos, a small TV and such—but Andrew didn't buy tickets for *that* raffle. He bought tickets where the prizes were a lop-eared dwarf rabbit, a guinea pig, and assorted hamsters. When I learned the truth, I knew without any shadow of a doubt that we held one of the winning tickets. In fact, we held two. That's how we ended up with another rabbit and a guinea pig. "Close your eyes," I said to Eric when we got home.

As a side note, as Flopsy, the adorable lop-eared dwarf rabbit, grew, she started to growl and look menacing whenever the boys cleaned out her cage. Eventually, they were too frightened to clean it, and so the job fell to me. I must admit, I, too, was terrified, but asking Eric to do it was out of the question. One day, when I reached into Flopsy's cage, not only did she growl, but she crouched down low and then attacked. With a yelp, I withdrew my hand only to find that she had sunk her teeth into the soft flesh of my palm. I tried to shake her free but the pain was excruciating.

I let out a blood curdling yell and Eric and the boys flew down the basement stairs. The children stopped in their tracks and stared in a sort of fascinated horror. "Do something, Dad," they cried from their vantage point of safety.

To his credit, Eric looked around and found a suitable weapon. Rolling up an old newspaper, he batted valiantly at the furry extension to my hand. "I'm not really sure," he screamed as he smacked at Flopsy, "exactly what the boys are supposed to learn from all this, Jen, or am I missing the obvious?" At last, Flopsy released her grip, fell onto the tattered basement carpet, and hopped away. Quickly, we all scrambled up the stairs to the kitchen and slammed the door.

Eric washed my hand and wrapped it in a towel. "What do we do now," he asked in his most sardonic voice, "use a chair and a whip to subdue her?"

I gave him a withering glance and called the breeder, who was most scornful when she learned that we had lacked the moral fiber necessary to establish ourselves as the alpha bunny. But she did agree to take away the marauding beast, along with Miniwhorewhore's offspring. All in all, Eric thought it had been rather a good day.

Now that most of the rabbits had disappeared, the house seemed woefully empty with just Mini and the guinea pig, and it wasn't long before the boys were bemoaning their fate.

"What they really want is a dog," Eric said one evening. "Perhaps if we get a dog," he reasoned, "they'll stop wanting more animals." I didn't like to point out the fallacy of his argument, but a dog would be nice, I agreed. Sherlock, a beagle puppy, moved in a few weeks later. The boys were thrilled but instead of stemming their desire, perversely, it took our animal husbandry to a whole new level.

Ben began to volunteer his time at the Little Red School House, a nature center close to our home. There then followed a range of refugee animals from the wild and a whole host of reptiles which took up residence in the basement: a hawk recovering from an injury to its wing, four baby sparrow hawks, various turtles, a number of snakes, and, following a visit to a reptile show, an iguana. I personally loved the iguana—by submerging her in a bath of warm water, we could make her poop. Since iguanas poop only once every five days or so, this meant she could roam the house freely, which she thoroughly enjoyed. Not so much Eric and Sherlock. Terrified, they clung to one another for moral support. It was the first time Eric had ever bonded with an animal.

But then, the local mouse population must have heard we were a boarding house of sorts. Mice flocked to our door like homing pigeons. Legions of mice moved in! I knew I had a real problem when I discovered that the bag of birdseed, which we kept in the utility room, was emptying at an alarming rate. In the crawl space, the mice were busy packing our suitcases with it—their insurance policy against a future famine. I couldn't help admiring their preparedness.

Conveniently, Eric had organized an extended business trip at the time, so I was left to deal with the problem alone. The plague delighted the boys who had created a log book and were diligently noting their sightings. At first, I set up non-lethal traps, "humane" affairs at which the mice scoffed. They felt so much at home that one afternoon as I watching an episode of *Nature*, I looked around and there was a grizzled old mouse sitting up on its haunches on the arm of the chair, watching the show with avid interest! I got up slowly but he didn't move—and I went into the kitchen for a paper towel. I came back and scooped him up. Taking him outside, I released him onto the lawn, when suddenly, a hawk swooped down and flew off with him. I'm ashamed to say I experienced a quiver of satisfaction.

When a mouse ran over me in bed on night, I finally drew the line. I considered the invasion of my bedroom an act of war. It never occurred to me to call Terminix®—this was personal. I purchased two dozen mouse traps, the old fashioned kind with the spring loader. That night I sat at the kitchen table rolling whole wheat bread and peanut butter into solid balls. I was humming to myself. Every now and then let out a low chuckle—there was something vaguely manic about my manner. Ben and Andrew gave me a wide berth.

"The trick, boys," I cackled, "is to bait the traps for a couple of nights, but not set them. Lull them into a false sense of security!"

The strategy worked—on the third morning most of the traps contained the corpse of a mouse. Donning rubber gloves, I threw both mice and traps into a large garbage bag and disposed of them. Remorse was a stranger to me. I purchased more traps. I was relentless and didn't rest until, at last, only one wily mouse remained. But no matter what traps I used or what stratagems I tried, the traps were sprung, the bait had disappeared, but the mouse escaped. The boys were thrilled and were clearly on his side. "Houdini lives!" they cried triumphantly each day when they checked the traps.

Gradually, even I developed a grudging respect for the cunning rodent. I began to realize that I had met my match, until one morning I found him on his back lying dead on the stairs. Blood trickled from the side of his mouth. Horrified, it dawned on me that he had been caught and had somehow freed himself from the trap. He must have died in dreadful agony. A wave of remorse washed over me. Gently, I wrapped my worthy opponent in paper towel. The least we could do was give our hero a decent burial. We buried Houdini under the apple tree beside his domesticated cousins, the gerbil and the hamster.

The strange thing was that when I went to gather up the traps, not one of them had been sprung, and I suddenly realized that Houdini had, in fact, died of natural causes. *What are the odds of that happening*, I thought to myself, but we all agreed that in some strange way it was a fitting end.

As is the way of the world, one by one our remaining

pets met their demise in various ways. Either the boys lost interest and the pets were given away, or they followed Houdini's example and died of natural causes. The boys, too, had grown up. Ben was at college and Andrew, the fireman, spent more time at the firehouse than at home.

The last to desert the fast emptying nest was our poor old dog, Sherlock. He had been ill for a long time, and we knew that soon the inevitable would happen. The boys were prepared for this and each had bid their faithful companion goodbye.

Sure enough, one afternoon I arrived home from work to find Sherlock in pitiful condition—it was winter time in Chicago, a blizzard howled and the roads were treacherous. There was no one else home but me; however, dangerous roads or no, I knew had no choice but to take him to the vet. Gently, I wrapped him in a blanket and made him comfortable on the back seat of the car. I had been to the opticians on my way home from work, and when I glanced in the rear view mirror, I saw that the whites of my eyes were still stained a bright orange from the drops they had used to dilate my pupils. There was nothing I could about this now.

I inched along through the blinding snow and finally made the turn into the vet's parking lot. Scooping Sherlock up and battling my way through the snow, I managed to reach the door, which flew open as I slid inside. Alarmed, the office assistant leaped to her feet, her hand pressed against her breast as if she feared I had a sub-machine gun concealed in the blanket. "It's Sherlock," I gasped.

"Oh, it's Mrs. Munro!" she said, relieved. "I hardly recognized you!"

I unbundled Sherlock. She took one look. "Oh, dear!" she whispered sadly. "Bring him right in. I'll get the vet." I went into the examining room. Soon, the vet arrived and told me to put Sherlock on the floor. Wobbling on his shaky legs, he took two or three steps toward the examining table where he managed to lift his leg and pee.

"His parting shot?" I asked, the tears beginning to spill from my orange eyes. She nodded silently. She left for a moment. Carefully, I cradled Sherlock in my arms. I kissed him and he licked my cheek. Then, the vet returned with the syringe, and I laid Sherlock on the examining table. I cupped his head in my hands, whispered nonsense words, and stroked him as she administered the fatal shot. Slowly, his eyes closed and his head and body went limp. I covered him in the blanket. "It was so peaceful," I whispered. "Will you do the same for me when it's my turn to go?" We looked at one another and smiled through our tears.

Somehow, I managed to get home. I called the boys and told them the bad news. Then, Eric arrived home from work. Immediately, he knew what had happened. He came toward me and took my face gently in his hands. An engineer by trade, he was not given to emotive endearments, but I knew this time *would* be different. Gently, he enfolded me in his arms. "There, there, Jen. It'll be all right. Shhsss, it'll be all right." All the time he patted my back. Of course, I began to sob in earnest. When I had wept my orange eyes back to white, I was able to look up at him at last and whisper, "Read my lips, Eric. No more pets!"

The Fisher King

THE FOUR WHITE VANS stood with their doors flung open, ready to accommodate the squealing teenagers, their sleeping bags, pillows, the step ladders, tool boxes, and assorted power tools. Every conceivable plumbing device, including, not only the kitchen sink but also a full-sized bath tub, lounged on the black top just daring us to find room for it.

We were off on a field trip to the mountains of East Tennessee to do general household repairs for people too poor or ill to do the work themselves. During the previous year, the senior high group and their leaders at our church had raised the six thousand dollars to fund the trip and buy the necessary supplies. We had taken workshops and learned how to hammer nails into wood and use power tools without maiming ourselves or others. Now we were being unleashed to practice our skills on the homes of the unsuspecting poor. I stood hopelessly looking at the supplies blanketing the church parking lot, doubtful we would be able to perform even the first miracle of making all of it disappear into the oversized vans that stood waiting.

With the eagerness endemic to youth, the teenagers threw the contents of the parking lot into the vans using neither logic, rhyme, nor reason. And miracle of miracles—they did the impossible. With the parking lot laid bare and black, we stood in a circle—hand in hand—with heads bowed as the pastor recited our "bon voyage" prayer. The only setback to our departure was caused by the Heineman's dog, Rusty, who, upon sniffing my farm-encrusted tennis shoes, lifted his leg, and relieved himself down mine. *A premonition of things to come,* I wondered ruefully to myself. And it was!

With humans loaded, the vans' engines and tape decks roared into life. In order to accommodate the variety of musical tastes on board our van, we listened to all kinds: heavy metal, light metal, soft rock, and hard rock then hip hop, be bop, rip rap, and clap trap. We listened to it all, including the favorite gospel hymn of my co-leader, Lemon-Drop Bob, "Shall We Gather at the River," no less than three times *each time he played it.* Bob, as his nickname suggests, consumed a vast amount of lemon drops on the journey. At last, having been a good sport, I now took out my Walkman and proceeded to listen to a special tape I had been saving for this moment. I put on my head phones and settled down to listen to Odds Bodkin tell the legend of *Percival and the Fisher*

King. Only five minutes into the story, I stopped the tape. "Listen, you guys!" No reaction. "Listen!" I shouted over the roar of the music. Bob turned it down.

"Oh God!" Someone groaned from the back. "She wants us to listen to a story!"

"Just listen for five minutes. If you don't like it, I'll go back to listening to it by myself. OK?"

They reluctantly agreed, and I started the tape. After a momentary crackle, we heard the melodious sound of a twelve-string guitar and the compelling voice of the storyteller weaving the Arthurian legend of Beloved Son, whose destiny is to ask the questions that will free the grail king from his enchantment. Beloved Son's real name is Percival, but his mother has kept his identity a secret, fearing she might lose him to a chivalrous death as she did her husband, Pellinore.

As the tale unfolded, no one in the van spoke. Lost in the mists of time, they listened intently as Beloved Son encounters a band of Arthur's knights, who laugh at this rustic; however, the damage has been done. He tells his mother he will become a knight of the round table. To foil his efforts, she sends him off wearing a thick, homespun woolen tunic that falls below his knees, a ludicrous fur hat with a long feather in it, and a huge pair of hairy boots. So absurd would Arthur's court find him that they would send him packing— but, of course, this does not happen.

As we listened, our van magically transformed into a white horse galloping toward a destiny that, unlike Percival, we hoped we might recognize. At last, the mountains of Tennessee loomed before us and we arrived at the school which would be our home for the next week. After unloading the vans and our belongings, we leaders set off to various sites to meet our families. Work would begin the next day, and we had to determine exactly what supplies we would need.

Lemon-Drop and I followed the directions which led us into the surrounding tree-covered mountains. We thought we knew what to expect, but nothing could have prepared us for the cold reality that shattered the magical stuff of legend. Sitting in a wheelchair on the porch, a legless, toothless old man grinned warmly. His wife, whose bare feet were red and swollen, waved to us excitedly. Before them, the garden was a tangled mess of wood, weeds, and rocks; a pervasive smell of sewage hung in the air.

After quickly introducing ourselves, we gazed over the porch railing at the beginnings of a wheelchair access ramp, which we would need to complete. The sweet, new wood smell was barely discernable in the stench. The old woman hobbled inside and we followed. I was appalled—not so much by the conditions themselves: the backed-up toilet, full to the brim with solid waste, the mounds of dirty clothes, the swarms of black flies that buzzed around half-eaten food left on the table, or the smell—but that no one was doing anything about it. And then it suddenly struck me that *we* were there to do something about it, and I was appalled even more.

We returned to the school in a subdued mood, but our

crew surrounded us eager to hear about "their" family. They were up for the challenge and helped load the van for an early start on Monday morning. Promptly at seven-thirty we left the school. Adam, who now called himself Beloved Son—which the kids shortened to BS—was in charge of morning devotions. Ignoring the script, he prayed, "Dear Lord, if it be your will that we meet the Fisher King on this our quest, inspire us to ask the right questions so that we can free him from his enchantment. Amen."

"We're not on a quest," Rocky said, "just a mission trip."

"Same thing," BS responded resolutely. Rocky sighed.

At Lemon-Drop's insistence we had all chosen nicknames for ourselves. In tribute to the Heineman's dog, I was now Rusty. Ryan, a short, skinny freshman, was Superman, Denise, Snow White, TJ, who never cracked a smile, was Joker, and Christine was Rocky.

As the van climbed the tortuous mountain road, the kids settled down and the tape deck roared to life. It wasn't long before we arrived at the small cabin where the old couple was seated as they had been the night before. They were grinning and waving, eager to meet this new band of helpers. As we looked down on the desolate little house—at the unfinished ramp, the tangled yard, and the flies, busy and thick, it was not so difficult to believe that this land, like that of the Fisher King, was in the grip of a curse, which had laid it waste.

"See," said BS, gesturing toward the old man, "there's

the king in his coracle. He dangles a length of twine into the muddied waters, but catches no fish. We're here to change that."

The others sighed but didn't say anything. BS took hold of the power saw, his golden sword perhaps, and led the charge from the van. He stood smiling before the astonished couple. Dressed as he was in a pair of oversized overalls, bright yellow boots, a wide-brimmed hat, a red bandanna tied jauntily around his neck, and a large pair of safety goggles, did he not look as foolish and eager as Percival when he arrives at Arthur's court?

"I come to champion the Lady Reagan," he cried. He laid the saw at the absent feet of the old man, untied his red bandanna, and gave it as tribute to the old woman. No explanation for this strange behavior seemed necessary. Laughing, Mrs. Reagan tied the bandanna around her arm and soon everyone was shaking hands and introducing themselves. Strangely enough, neither the old man nor the old woman asked why we all bore such odd names, but this was not their destiny, nor was it their time for questions.

Immediately, we split into three groups: Snow White and Superman began to dig out a rock that was obstructing the pathway of the ramp. Lemon-Drop, Rocky, and Joker started to measure and cut the wood into the necessary lengths for the ramp. Meanwhile, BS and I tackled the toilet—lucky us!

In a flurry of enthusiasm, we set to work. Flies buzzed blissfully around us as we dismantled the toilet, slid a board beneath it, and then carried it—oh, so carefully—through the treacherous obstacle course of the front yard. The relentless heat of the Tennessee sun illuminated the contents as we dumped it into a ditch. Then, we returned to the bathroom to remove the rotted floor.

As we worked, the old man wheeled his chair into the doorway to watch our progress. BS peppered him with questions and the answers were forthcoming. We learned the old couple had one grown son. Mrs. Reagan shuffled into the house to get a photograph. "Here," she said proudly holding it up so we could admire her husband, who had legs and teeth, and the small, serious boy, who gripped his father's hand and stared at the camera.

"Do you get to see him much?" BS continued, but the old man didn't answer. Instead, he wheeled himself back to the porch; the old woman's eyes filled with sudden tears. "No, not much," she whispered before an uncomfortable silence fell. BS stood up and put his arms around her.

At lunchtime, we retired to the shade of the one small tree in the front yard. Superman and Snow White constructed makeshift seats out of the planks of wood. Wrapping our hands in plastic bags, we devoured our sandwiches. The smell of raw sewage, which still hung heavily in the air, did nothing to dampen our appetites. For suburban kids, they had come a long way.

Rocky settled next to BS. "So, you seem to be getting to know the Reagans? Asking the right questions?"

"I'm trying. But it's hard. I kind of understand why Percival didn't ask the questions the first time he went to the castle. You know, why the spear dripped blood, what ailed the king, and how the grail magically fed everyone."

"Yes, but that was because of the stupid old knight who told him not to ask too many questions, right?"

BS replied, "I know, but questions cause pain. It's just not that easy."

After lunch we labored through the hottest hours of the day, and the progress of the morning became a fond memory. The rock impeding the path of the ramp had grown into a bolder and when we removed the bathroom floor, we discovered why the toilet had backed up. The plastic sewer pipe lay on its side and had huge gaping holes down its length. Finally, BS, whose constant questions were slowly driving everyone but the Reagans nuts, broke the blade of the power saw. We had no replacement.

"OK, it's almost four o'clock. Let's determine what supplies we'll need tomorrow and head back."

"A stick of dynamite might be useful," suggested Snow White sweetly.

Since we had turned off the water, we made sure the Reagans had enough to last them until the next day. On the way back, we stopped off to pick up the supplies we would need and returned to the school. After a hot shower and meal, it wasn't long before we collapsed into our beds—ready to fight another day.

The next morning on the way to our site, Superman led devotions according to script, but added his own ending. "And if it be your will, inspire BS to keep asking the right questions so that we find the Holy Grail. Amen"

When we arrived, the Fisher King and the Grail Maiden, as we were now calling the old man and his wife, were in exactly the same positions as they had been on our first day. The Grail Maiden untied the bandanna from around her arm and waved it cheerily. Our intrepid band of teenagers responded in kind, and after a brief conversation, immediately set to work.

Superman and Joker tackled the boulder, BS and Snow White sawed more wood—not only for the ramp but also for the bathroom floor. In the bathroom Rocky and Lemon Drop removed the defunct hot water heater. Meanwhile, I crawled under the house to start removing the sewer pipes—*like the kids, I, too, had come a long way.*

After only about an hour, I heard an unearthly yell. It was BS. "I've done it again! I've broken the golden blade!"

"Hey, don't worry about it," yelled Lemon-Drop. "I'll get the replacement; you give a hand with the rock.

Superman and Joker had thrown a strong rope around the boulder and all the kids, laughing, took hold of the end. As they pulled, the Fisher King and the Grail Maiden, taking us by surprise, began to sing. Their oddly stirring voices filled the air: "Yo, heave oh! Yo, heave ho! Once more, once again, still once more."

The kids joined in with the next chorus of "yo, heave ohs" and as if defeated by the magical singing, the boulder leaped from the ground.

The Fisher King and Grail Maiden cheered, and then she hobbled off toward the kitchen. BS joined the old man and they both talked earnestly until she returned with a battered tray on which rested an assortment of chipped cups and a plate of home-made biscuits. Strictly speaking, we were not allowed take food or drink from our families, who had so little, but no one chose to remember the rule. As the old woman handed out the simple fare, Rocky whispered, "And each took meat and drink to his own liking, and all were satisfied." Gratefully, we drank the lemonade and sank our teeth into the tender biscuits; we had never tasted such sweet ambrosia before.

"Get the box," the old man told his wife abruptly. We were surprised by his tone, and so was she. Nonetheless, she disappeared inside and returned carrying a cereal box. With trembling fingers, the old man took it and with a sadness we could not fathom, dug deep inside. He fished out a gold watch, which he handed to BS.

"It's beautiful," he murmured, brushing the cereal dust from its surface.

"It belonged to my grandfather who passed it down to my father who passed it down to me." He stopped for a moment, as if the next words were lodged in his throat. At length he continued, "Someday, I should like to pass it along to our boy." At this, the tears flowed in a steady stream down his cheeks.

For once, BS could find no words of comfort. In the silence that followed, the membrane between myth and reality dissolved. We gazed reverently upon the Holy Grail in BS's hands. Slowly, he returned it to the old man who held it close to his heart before he buried it once more inside the cereal box.

When we packed up for the day and left, the Reagans sat on their porch. They waved but didn't have the heart to smile and neither did we.

The next day, as if by magic, we galloped along with our projects: the ramp grew at an amazing rate and the plumber Lemon-Drop had managed to find was busy installing the new polyurethane sewer pipe. At this rate, we might be able to turn the water back on, which was what we wanted more than anything. Toward the end of the week, the plumber had finished installing the sewer pipes, Lemon-Drop had hooked up the new water heater, and the ramp was nearly completed. Now all we needed was a new toilet, which was the only stumbling block to our plans to turn on the water. The tiny building supply store in town had one cracked toilet in stock. They assured us they were expecting a delivery any day and failed to understand our impatience.

On our last morning, which promised to be another scorching day, we absorbed the fact that we had failed in our mission and the next team would have the privilege of turning on the water. The Reagans, who had not complained once about the absence of a toilet, seemed content to use whatever they had devised in its stead. Despite our disappointment, we finished the ramp and sanded the rails before cleaning up the yard and the house.

At last, our work was done. We were amazed at the transformation. It was not quite as dramatic as the one at the Fisher King's castle, which was mythical in scale. Nonetheless, as we looked around at the house, clean and tidy, and the yard, free of debris, we were pleased with the magic we had wrought. We said our goodbyes and promised to return at four o'clock to pick them up for the celebratory picnic to be held at the school.

As promised, we arrived a little before four behind the handicapped-accessible van, which would transport the Reagans. The couple waited on the porch. Their smiling faces shone and they wore their Sunday best. We, too, had changed into the one good outfit we each had brought for this occasion.

To our surprise, another van arrived. It was the plumber! He stuck his head out of the window. "Open the back!" he shouted excitedly. The kids did so and to their immense delight discovered a toilet. "Just don't ask where I got it!" he shouted with a laugh. With a great cheer, the kids carried it aloft—as if it were a golden throne.

"It won't take long to connect," the plumber announced, as he and Lemon-Drop disappeared into the house. Soon, they reappeared, "All set."

"A ceremonial flush!" yelled BS, grabbing the handles of the old man's wheel chair. Laughing, everyone followed and crowded into the small bathroom. The old man looked at his wife. "Go on, then!" he cried.

As if she were about to take hold of the Holy Grail itself, she leaned forward reverently and depressed the lever. We held our collective breath. After a momentary burble and gurgle of air bubbles and spitting water, a swollen stream swirled around and around, ending in a satisfying gulp and burp. In our minds, we could see the green fields sweeping across the king's barren landscape, the trees bursting into their green foliaged finery, the birds flying through the sunlit sky, and the fish leaping in the sparking blue waters of the river.

Moved by the moment, our small band broke into song, Lemon-Drop's favorite, and we didn't mind singing it three times!

> *Shall we gather at the river,*
> *Where bright angel feet have trod,*
> *With its crystal tide forever*
> *Flowing by the throne of God?*

Yes, we will gather at the river,
The beautiful, the beautiful river;
Gather with the saints at the river
That flows by the throne of God. [13]

Laughing and singing, we assembled on the porch and watched the van driver push the old man in his wheelchair down the ramp. His wife walked beside him. When they reached the bottom, the old man looked back at us—and like a prize fighter—clasped his hands above his head in a victory salute.

BS cupped his mouth with his hands and shouted, "Now you can go fishing again!"

Whether the old man had ever fished before in his life, we didn't know, but he took hold of an imaginary fishing rod and cast it expertly into the air. Then, he clasped his wife's hands, kissed them, and whispered hoarsely, "We'll go fishing for our boy, Mother."

We all had tears in our eyes as—before he disappeared into the van—the Fisher King once more cast his imaginary line into the healing waters of mystical time.

---

13   From the hymn "Shall We Gather at the River?" By Robert Lowry, 1864.

Acknowledgements

I WOULD FIRST LIKE TO THANK BILL NAUGHTON whose collection of short stories about ordinary, working class people called *The Goal Keeper's Revenge* inspired me to write my own family and childhood stories.

Carol Birch has also earned my gratitude for her unswerving friendship, for generously sharing her considerable expertise, and for listening so profoundly and deeply to my work. Most of all, however, I wish to thank her for her support in getting these stories published. Without her, this would not have happened.

I would also like to thank Odds Bodkin, that magical storyteller described by *Billboard* magazine as being "a modern day Orpheus," for giving me permission to use his name and his story "Percival and the Fisher King," which informed and inspired my short story, "The Fisher King."

I owe a debt of gratitude to Doug Lipman for his perceptive insights and constructive advice. Like a gentle-hearted mentor, he praised the triumphs; like an eagle-eyed teacher, he honed in on the weaknesses and then never failed to cheer the revisions.

Finally, last but by no means least, I would like to thank my husband, Eric, for his sharp editorial eye and his unfailing love, and my two sons, Benjamin and Andrew, for their enthusiastic support and love.

Reading Group Extras

Author's Essay

MY STORIES HAVE EMERGED from the fragmented moments of my personal history. When my mother related to me that a Romany gypsy had prophesized her life would come to an end when she was forty-three, all the magical moments of my childhood came into sharp focus. Suddenly, I understood why she had told us play is children's work, why we didn't have to do any chores around the house—a fact I have never revealed to my own children—and why she devoted herself so tirelessly to loving my father and her four children. It provided the perfect frame for the story "Sundays," which is a story about loss and love and prophecy.

Placing my father at the center of this story, I then brought to mind all the anecdotes I could remember about him and realized that many of them took place on a Sunday. In looking back, I discovered there was a ritualistic quality to our Sundays, which had an underlying rhythm that allowed me to thread the different anecdotes together so that they form the arc of a satisfying narrative.

This raises the interesting question of what makes a story. In school, we are told that all stories introduce a conflict, a problem to be solved, which sets in motion a number of actions that lead to a climax in which the problem is resolved and then the story concludes with the denouement. Donald Davis, in his book *Telling Your Own Stories*, adds an additional element, which I think is crucial—it corresponds to the idea of theme. Davis says that the "crisis[14]" or climax must lead to what he calls a moment of "insight" in which the main character learns something important about himself, someone else, or the world. It is critical to the creation of a satisfactory story and it must resonate with our audience.

In "Sundays" the moment of insight occurs when we four children discover the source of strength that will give us the resilience to go on with our lives despite the loss of my father.

The lovely thing about writing stories as opposed to writing memoir is that one is not tied to the relentless constraints of linear time. One can play fast and loose with chronology. It's more important to find connection: how do anecdotes relate thematically rather than *when* they happened in relation to one another. This was the case with "Aunty

14.   A crisis, according to Donald Davis, is "any happening which takes a part of our lives with which we are comfortable and turns it upside down so that we have to adjust to a world that is shaped differently than before."

Lily." On Sunday afternoons, Aunty Lily and Uncle Harry came over for tea. On one such Sunday, she related the fact that she had been waiting at the bus stop when the elastic in her underwear had broken. We all thought this was hilarious and it became part of our family folklore.

On another Sunday, my mum and Aunty Lily went for a walk and were caught in a downpour. On their return, Aunty Lily proceeded to repair the damage wrought by the storm. As she took herself apart, we four children sat at the kitchen table watching her. When the deconstruction was complete, she turned and gave us the benefits of her succinct distillation of what is important in life, a lesson we never forgot. In creating the story "Aunty Lily," it seemed natural to me to put these two memorable anecdotes together and to put myself in the story. Does the story suffer because it does not adhere rigidly to the "facts"? No! On the contrary, it is improved—or at least—I think so, because it provides such important insight into the human condition. It's a lovely story on so many levels.

So, finding thematic connection among anecdotes is one way I create story. Another method I use is the journey motif as described by Joseph Campbell in his book *The Hero With a Thousand Faces*. Simply put, the hero receives the call to adventure—she must go on a journey to solve a problem that only she can solve. She has help in the form of a protective figure and is given an amulet to use to overcome the obstacles in her quest. Such is the case with "The Wicket Gate," which chronicles my difficulties learning to read. The structure of this story not only includes elements of the hero journey but also follows the journey motif implicit in the allegory *The Pilgrim's Progress* by John Bunyan, which Miss Turner reads to us daily. It is in its own right a hero journey. Just as Christian's call to adventure is to follow the straight and narrow path leading to the wicket gate, a portal through which he must pass in order to reach the Celestial City, so I, too, set out as Pilgrim toward my own wicket gate of learning to read. Only then will I find the Celestial City—the whole world of books that suddenly becomes available together with a future that now has infinitely more potential.

So the journey motif provided the structure for this story; however, the motivation to write it came from a simple desire to honor a beloved teacher and capture the magic of my primary school experience. I attended a public school whose curriculum was based on the educational theories of Pestalozzi, a Swiss educational reformer. His motto was "Learning by head, hand, and heart." Our classroom held large sand and water trays, huge wooden building blocks, a play house, a table for modeling clay, and a nature table. Though many of these features do not appear in my story; nonetheless, they lend their magic to the tone of the story and Miss Turner certainly supplies the loving application of Pestalozzi's philosophy. Above all else, Miss Turner devoted herself to the supreme task of developing our imaginations.

I think there is really only one motivation behind many of my stories: I set out trying to capture the magic of things, especially my childhood, a childhood in which we were free to roam, explore, fight and settle our own arguments, and play. I loved the games we played—we never played organized sports, neither did we play sports out in the street. We played the traditional games that generations of kids had played before us—tin-tin-ta-lurky, British Bulldog, conkers, stilts, snobs, winter warmers. It's where I learned the inviolate code of fair play. I also wanted to capture the magic of living in a large family in a small house, the magic of living with my granddad, the joy of having two funny, loving parents, who rarely spoke the words "I love you," which were never necessary. All this, I hope, comes out in my stories.

Since my stories are created for performance, there must of necessity be a simplicity about them: I do not dwell too much on developing characters' internal emotional landscapes. My descriptions cannot be too long or detailed. However, in the storytelling community, my stories are probably considered a little too literary when compared to the oral style of other tellers. I think there is a reason for this: I grew up listening to BBC radio where I heard short stories, plays, the *Goon Show*, *Round the Horn*, and a rich variety of panel shows in which story and clever word play, puns, and limericks were standard fare. They were a treasure trove of rich, complex language, which I unconsciously absorbed. And because there were no visuals, I fell in love with the spoken word. (I was also significantly deaf as a young child, and when this problem was corrected, the impact of being able to hear language easily totally transfixed me.)

One of my early influences was Joyce Grenfell, a sophisticated comedian who performed a series of humorous monologues. Her characterizations of both upper and lower class people were poignantly accurate and provided little slices of life that revealed broad insights into the British character. I especially loved her language, which was complex and rich and bold. She appeared on television as well as radio, so she spanned these two media and united them for me. However, even on television her performances were storytelling at its finest.

I like to think that my language also has a richness to it—I love description and feel it's important to convey setting and action as vividly as possible. I especially like the description of Miss Hacket—the Hatchet! This image of a hatchet is continued throughout the scene in which she is introduced and combines with images of ice: "She sliced into the room and eyed us suspiciously." "Her eyes were slits, her nose a meat cleaver." "The words fell out of her mouth like shards of ice." I think they help bring the scene and the Hatchet into sharp focus.

Finally, writing for me is a mystical process. When I have an idea for a story, I let it sit with me for a while; I mull over the ideas and when I am performing a mindless task such as doing the ironing or the laundry, images leap fully formed from the subconscious. I "see" the story as it unfolds in my mind. I do not judge, but simply watch as it unfolds. Writing then becomes so much easier because all I need to do is write what I have seen. When I am stuck and cannot see the way to end a story or fashion a scene, I surrender the problem to the universe. I let it sit in my subconscious, and soon the solution arrives in a series of vivid mental images.

All this sounds deceptively easy and effortless, but it isn't. A great deal of fear and many questions accompany the process: *Will the images come? Will the universe finally desert me? Will everyone eventually discover I have no talent?* In answer, I can only say that a significant amount of trust and patience are required and so far it hasn't let me down.

Biography

JENNIFER MUNRO WAS BORN IN THURMASTON, a small English village just outside the busy industrial town of Leicester. Thurmaston is filled with working class people who have generous hearts, a grammatically incorrect and discordantly musical accent, and a gift for storytelling. This is where she fell in love with the spoken word.

She attended Bangor Normal College, North Wales, where she earned a bachelor's degree in education, her main subjects being dramatic art and English literature. Steeped in the musical language of Wales, she unconsciously absorbed a love of Celtic music, spoken word, and the rich folklore of this mythical land.

After graduating, she taught English Literature and drama in a London high school before marrying her husband Eric and immigrating to the United States in 1976. They settled in Illinois where they raised two boys. Jennifer taught seventh and eighth grade English for a while, and then she discovered storytelling. She was invited into her son's second grade classroom to read a story, but Jennifer opted to learn the story and tell it orally. The effect on the children was dramatic: they listened so intently and so profoundly it was quite clear that something very magical was happening.

In that moment, the seed of storytelling had been sown! Jennifer began searching collections of fairy and folktales, picture books, and legends to find stories for her incipient repertoire and began telling stories professionally in schools and libraries.

When Jennifer discovered that storytelling was undergoing a renaissance in the United States, she attended festivals all over the country and fell in love with the personal story. However, it took a while before she found the courage to create and write her own stories. The various influences of living in a large, chaotic family in a working class village combined with the magical experience of living in Wales translated into a repertoire of personal and mythical stories that resonate with the frailty and resilience of the human experience. Populated with memorable characters that spring vividly to life, her stories take the reader on a roller coaster ride of emotions that elicits both laughter and tears. Syd Lieberman wrote of her work: "A good storyteller should move you emotionally and be able to transport you to another time and place. Jennifer's stories do just that."

Jennifer moved to Connecticut in 2002 where she taught eighth grade English in Madison, the town where she now lives with her husband, Eric. Joseph Campbell's book *The Hero with a Thousand Faces* formed the basis of the curriculum and this allowed Jennifer to apply her storytelling skills in the classroom. During this time she earned a master's degree in Oral Traditions from the Graduate Institute. She also continued with her storytelling career, especially creating and writing stories.

Jennifer has performed her stories at festivals across the nation, most notably at the National Storytelling Festival in Jonesborough, Tennessee, at the Timpanogos Storytelling Festival in Utah, at the University of San Diego Adult Storytelling Concert series, at the Connecticut Storytelling Festival, and at the Cape Girardeau Storytelling Festival in Missouri. She has produced two award winning CDs. The magazine *Storytelling World* selected the story "Aunty Lily" from *Relatives and their Body Parts* as a winner in the category of Stories for Adult Listeners. Her CD *Beginnings*, a collection of touching and hilarious stories about giving birth, was also a winner in the same category.

Q&A with Jennifer Munro

Q Are you a storyteller or a writer?

A Yes! I tell the stories I write. In other words, I perform my stories live before an audience. I do not create my stories orally, but write them first. When I rehearse them, I modify them by "rounding out the corners" of the written text so that they "sound" more like natural language. In writing the stories first, I find the richness of the detail; the oral telling reveals the rhythm of the words and the internal rhythm of the story.

Q How did your family life set you on this path of being a storyteller/story writer?

A Many of my close relatives were—and continue to be—exceptional rogues, gossipers, and raconteurs. On Sunday afternoons when Aunty Lily and Uncle Harry visited, story and gossip spilled across the creaky kitchen table. We children, making sure we could be seen but not heard, listened in rapt attention, soaking up the images and details of the lives of the saints and sinners who populated our family and neighborhood. These details and fragments formed the raw material of what grew into my stories.

Q How did your neighborhood impact the stories you create?

A In every way! It was a scrappy, working class neighborhood and some of the kids were tough. Like most kids of that time, we were left to our own devices. In an era before organized sports—or organized anything—we played our own games: whip and top, marbles, conkers, stilts, kick-the-can, and tin-tin-ta-lurky. We transitioned from one to the other according to an invisible, cyclical rhythm. On dark nights under the light of the green street lamp in the cul-de-sac, which we called "the ring," we congregated in this magical underworld with its own, unique hierarchical power structure. It was sometimes frightening, occasionally dangerous, but always intoxicating.

QWhat prompted you to begin to create stories?

At festivals across the nation, storytellers told personal stories, but I was convinced I had no suitable material from which to craft stories. Instead, I told myths, legends, fairy tales, and three literary stories from a collection of short stories called *The Goal Keeper's Revenge* by Bill Naughton, who is best known for writing the play *Alfie*. Bill's stories resonated with me because they are about ordinary, working class people. Bill kindly gave me permission to tell three of them. However, as much as I loved and still love these stories, they belong to Bill; they resonate with Bill's reality, not mine. But the daring question had been planted in my mind—if Bill could write stories about ordinary people, why couldn't I?

QDo you have what might be termed a "signature" story? What makes it quintessentially yours?

A"Aunty Lily" is that story for me; it was the first story I ever wrote. In contrast to many of my stories, it's relatively short, but it contains so much. A beautiful woman loses her underwear in public; thus, in a way she becomes exposed and vulnerable. At the climax of the story, she deconstructs herself and in so doing chooses to become exposed and vulnerable. This is her strength and this is what I learned from her as a result. I also happened to learn the more obvious life lessons stated directly in the story: beauty is only skin deep, things are never what they seem, and conscientious tooth care will be rewarded.

Q How do your stories come into being? How do you transform them from idea to story?

A I remember snatches, images, moments, or stories from my past. I can "see" all the characters vividly in my mind. I remember so much—much of it first hand and much of it through family stories that provided our identity as a family. From this rich stew of experience, I pull out the details of my stories. At one time, once I had an idea for a story, I would rush immediately to the computer and begin work on it. Now, I wait. I put the ideas, questions, images, characters into the back of my mind and allow them to simmer. Then, when I am doing something quite mindless, images will form in my head—and I quite literally "see" the story unfold like a movie. The writing process becomes so much easier this way.

Q How did your struggle learning to read help or hinder your ability to create and write stories?

A Ironically, it was critical to my ability to create and see images. My difficulties were many: I couldn't separate my left hand from my right. I inverted letters, transposed them, and wrote them upside down or backwards. Every now and then, I still write the number 3 instead of an S. Moreover, as a result of chronic ear infections, I was also significantly deaf. This combination of challenges forced me to pay close attention to the world: to notice the nuances of facial expressions and "read" the subtext of what was going on. Thus, the world was made more vivid. Then, when I did learn to read, it arrived in one shattering bolt from the blue! Suddenly, the unknown revealed itself in vibrant worlds filled with vivid images as tangible as the realities of home and family, school and friends.

Q How important is humor in your stories?

A One might as well ask if humor is important to life; without it, bits and pieces of us wither and die. The question: what makes some things funny fascinates me. From Plato and Aristotle to Freud, many have tried to come up with a theory that answers this question, none of them totally successfully. Today, many experts subscribe to some form of incongruity theory: an inconsistency exists between what is expected and what actually happens. For example, no one expects Miss Turner's bosoms to be anything other than fluid. However, at the climactic moment in the story when they "sat rigidly to attention, as O. Henry would say like 'two setters at the scent of a quail'" the unexpectedness of this action is humorous. However, expecting that something will happen and having that expectation confirmed can also be deliciously funny. For instance, in the scene when my father, wearing hair rollers, answers the door to the "leader of the conservative, moral right." We expect Mrs. Whistle-botham to be horrified and we are not disappointed. In this example, the reader enjoys the satisfaction of being right. The general consensus is that comedy is more difficult to write than tragedy. If people do laugh at my stories, it emanates from the recognition of our shared human fallibility.

Q What are the important craft techniques that you employ to create your stories? How do they help shape the story?

A I love simile, metaphor—particularly extended metaphor—especially personification when inanimate objects become involved in the action, which can so often lead to humor. It can also deepen the poignancy of the moment. I am also passionate about the rhythm of words—for example, "My aunty Lily bought for me a pair of black patent leather, silver buckled, totally unsuitable—I'll never be allowed in town with Aunty Lily again—school shoes!" This is not poetry but I like to think that it has a lyrical quality and that is important in writing.

Q Many of your stories are first person narratives. How closely are these stories inspired by real people and real events?

A Most events described in my stories are inspired by "real" events I experienced directly or indirectly through shared family folklore. The stories we shared as a family contained moments at which I was present, but which I don't actually remember because I was too young. However, they are still my stories. Therefore, by extension, all stories about other family members, friends, and relatives become potential grist for my narrative mill. They are "authentic" because they resonate with the truth of my experience.

Q On a related question, how do you transform your life experiences into a satisfying story and at the same time maintain the trust of the reader?

A It is incumbent upon me to shape the raw material of my experience into a story that not only has a satisfying narrative arc but also conveys some meaningful understanding about the human condition. In order to do this, I must, in the words of Nathaniel Hawthorne, "exercise some latitude in fashioning the work and the material." However, latitude is not license. If I take too many liberties, I risk losing the trust of my reader.

Q Many authors have a fear of the blank page. Have you ever experienced this type of fear?

A Yes, often! When I have an idea for a story and I have let it simmer for a while, there comes a time when I must begin to write. This is terrifying! It's a complex fear made up of much insecurity: Will I somehow fail the story? Will the story elude me? Will I fail to measure up? Then, once I have overcome the fear and completed the story, there is also the recurrent fear that I will be unable to create another.

Q Once you have written a story, does it remain frozen on the page or is it still open to change?

A Stories are fluid creations. In a live performance the unfolding story is a co-creation between teller and audience. For example, some parts of a story may need more detailed explanation, while other parts require less. The audience's laughter may prompt improvisation revealing a nuance in the story which did not exist previously—but adds to its richness.

If you have enjoyed Jennifer Munro's stories,
please take some time to visit:

www.jenniemunro2015.wordpress.com
www.parkhurstbrothers.com
www.storynet.org